COMANCHE WELCOME

And so we kept on arguin' like that for a minute when all of a sudden a shot whistled over our heads. We all spun around with our guns drawn in the direction it came from, and there, sittin' on horseback on a little grassy hill above us, was about twenty Comanche warriors, all pointin' their rifles at us. One of 'em yelled somethin' and made a motion that we knowed meant "drop your guns or we'll fill you full of lead." We obliged, of course, and soon they had us roped and were pullin' us back toward the village.

———◆———

BURN THE BREEZE

JACK BRENNAN

HarperPaperbacks
A Division of HarperCollinsPublishers

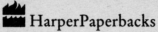 HarperPaperbacks

A Division of HarperCollins*Publishers*
10 East 53rd Street, New York, N.Y. 10022-5299

This is a work of fiction. The characters, incidents, and dialogues are products of the author's imagination and are not to be construed as real. Any resemblance to actual events or persons, living or dead, is entirely coincidental.

ISBN 0-06-101164-4

HarperCollins®, 🏛 ®, and HarperPaperbacks™
are trademarks of HarperCollins*Publishers*, Inc.

Cover illustration by Antonio Gabrielle

First printing: April 1997

Printed in the United States of America

Visit HarperPaperbacks on the World Wide Web at
http://www.harpercollins.com/paperbacks

❖ 10 9 8 7 6 5 4 3 2 1

This book is dedicated to my wife, without whom
nothing would ever get done,
and whose eyes,
quite apart from their ebony gleam,
speak to me of what's mine
that was once but my dream.

ACKNOWLEDGMENTS

The author wishes to thank the editor of this book, Jessica Lichtenstein, whose patience and understanding went far beyond the call of duty. I would also like to thank my parents for their cherished support over the years.

1

This story ain't about me. The story of my life ain't worth the telling, just the part of it that concerns a man named Abel Braddock—that's who this is really about. But I figured since I'm doing the talking, you should know a little about me and how I come to be associated with Mr. Braddock. So here goes.

My name is Boyd McKenzie and I was born in 1843, on a ship, of all places, halfway between Liverpool and Boston. Ma and Pa were on their way from Scotland to go live with Pa's brother, who had a store in a little Texas town called Vearden, which was near to Fort Worth. My folks didn't plan on my being born at sea like that; they figured they had another month yet. Anyway, we moved in with Uncle Malcolm for a year till Pa got us a little shack of our own—and I do mean shack, you know, one of them soddies that leaked like crazy when it rained. But it was home, and, being a kid who didn't know any better, I reckon I would've been happy any place.

Well, I was six years old when a coupla wagon loads of men drove past on their way out to California to dig for gold—you know, the big rush back in the late forties. I remember thinking those men looked like they were having the time of their lives, and when Pa told me they were headed west to dig for gold, I decided right then that I had to become a gold prospector, too. Didn't even know what gold was, but it sure had a nice ring to it, and it seemed to me those men were awful happy on account of it—'course, I realize now they were probably just drunk. Still, it was enough to make them fellers jump into wagons and ride through some rough Indian territory to go and get. So when I was eighteen, I was just about to set out myself when the damn war started up. I didn't know any more about the war than I did about gold, but every feller I knew had joined up already, so that settled that.

I still remember those first few weeks in the army like they were yesterday—most fun I ever had in my life, I reckon—but that was only 'cause the fighting hadn't started yet. They gave us brand-new uniforms, our very own guns, and, well, for a while we just sorta stood around admiring ourselves, speculating very optimistically about the way things would turn out.

'Course, all the yammering stopped once we got a taste of the real thing. During my first set-to with the enemy, the man next to me got shot, and it seemed like everything moved real slow for a few seconds. I remember seeing clear as day that he was dead before he even hit the ground. Nothing ever looked as dead as that man laying there. Well, from then on I was just plain scared of dying all the time. At least, I was until Abel Braddock come along.

What happened was, about a year into the war our commanding officer got killed and they replaced him with this young Lieutenant Braddock. Now, I'll tell you right up front that, at first, he was the sorriest commander a soldier ever had. Most of us were pretty young, but back then Abel looked like he had just stepped out from behind his mama's petticoats for the first time. We all figured they must be getting mighty short of the real thing if he was the best they could send. But, I swear to you, within a month the whole regiment would've followed Lieutenant Braddock off a cliff, if that's where he was going. And you know why? 'Cause we knew he'd always find a way to get most of us through alive somehow. He was that good.

Well, it didn't seem like it was ever gonna end, that war, but finally it did, and those of us with no families to go home to were trying to figure out what to do with ourselves when we heard that Abel, who the Yankee high command had no end of respect for, got permission to organize a special detachment of ex-confederate soldiers to go fight Indians under his command. So me and a few of the other men decided to volunteer to go with him, and the Union army, well, they were only too happy to oblige. When the Colonel found out—he was a colonel by then—he came over to meet us volunteers and we all became friends, me, Colonel Braddock, John Waldron, Horace Dobbs, Bill Evans, and Lem Massey.

You couldn't have handpicked half a dozen guys less likely to hit it off than the six of us. Lem Massey, for instance, he was thinking of becoming a preacher before the war broke out, but once the shooting started he became about the most ungodly man you could imagine, and he never looked back, as they say. Lem was tall and skinny, and always looked like he was mad as hell about something, which more often than not was the case.

Horace Dobbs, now he was a real educated type, you know, from money, but you didn't hold it against him 'cause he didn't show off and he was always making jokes about himself. He was a real hoot, and even when I had no idea what he was talking about I found myself laughin' at him. And if you wanted to see his ornery side, all you had to do was call him Horace to his face. His family owned a whole lotta property in Georgia, but Dobbsy couldn't stand the high life and just took off west one day, windin' up in Texas eventually, just in time to enlist.

Bill Evans, well, he had about ten diff'rent jobs before he wound up doing a stretch in prison for killing a man over a game of poker. Ugly as sin, but a nice enough feller once you got to know him. He had some education, too, and spoke about as well as Dobbsy. Anyway, he and Abel was the only ones who seemed to understand Dobbs half the time. He was also awful good to have around in a tight spot. So was John Waldron, on account of he was big and tough. Johnny was kinda like me at the time, a hayseed who didn't know which end was up, but with Johnny it wasn't just that he was green—he must have been about the dumbest man that ever lived. To give you an idea, Johnny thought the sun and the moon were the same thing! Now, personally, I can't tell you much about either one, but I sure as hell could always tell the two apart.

And what was Colonel Braddock like? Well, he was one of them sorta people you can see right away are different. Now me, I reckon I was a good enough looking feller, at least for the likes of the women I come across. But Abel had a sort of, well, a glow about him, I guess you could say. Everybody wanted to be his friend as soon as they met him. I seen Abel just talk his way outta getting killed more than a few times, but he was also real fast and real accurate with a gun—pistol, rifle, cannon, whatever was handy.

As for women, well, the few women around Abel during the time I knew him all kinda threw themselves at him, which he didn't mind one bit. And every man that knew him respected him— you had to. Abel Braddock was a brave and just man who never did anybody wrong who didn't have it coming. He was always as good as his word, which is something you really appreciated when you were in harm's way a lot of the time like we were. Dobbs used to call him things like "Good King Abel" and "Abel the Lionheart" behind his back.

So anyhow, off we went to the Dakota Territory to fight Sioux. It was like learning about war for the first time all over again, 'cause the Sioux were nothing like the Yankees we'd been fighting. Not to take nothing away from the Yankee soldiers, mind you, but your average Sioux Indian is about the toughest sonofabitch in all of God's creation. And the way he comes at you, all covered in paint and hollering like a banshee—even us hardened veterans felt a little uneasy the first time we heard that infernal yelling—didn't sound like men at all. During the war, you heard all sorts of carrying on in the heat of battle, but nothing like that. And, like I said, they were tough.

Colonel Braddock told us to take our time drawing a bead on a Sioux, 'cause an arm or leg shot wouldn't even slow him down. He was exaggerating some on that point, 'cause once I personally took down a great big one that way—hit him square in the thigh and down he went, roaring like a bull-calf. But believe me, I wasn't *aiming* for his thigh. I always did like the Colonel said.

One of the hardest things was getting used to wearing that damn Yankee-style uniform. It was actually more comfortable than our confederate getup, and I for one thought I looked better in blue, but for the first few months we was all scared we'd forget during a scrape and start shooting at each other outta habit. But you get used to just about anything in this life, and pretty soon we was polishing them brass buttons like we'd never worn nothin' else.

Well, the six of us somehow got through a few years of fighting Indians—mind you, not years of fighting for your life all the time, like in the war. In fact, you don't know what boredom is till you spend some time patrollin' around a wooden fort out in the middle of nowhere, waiting on some renegade Indians that never showed up. At first I used to dream about being attacked by Indians, then wake up safe and sound, and all disappointed.

But once things got going, we all really hated the Indian campaigns. Some, like Dobbs and Evans, didn't like it 'cause they admired the Sioux deep down and felt we ought to leave them be. No one called them Indian-lovers, though, 'cause they didn't let their opinions interfere with them doing their jobs, which sometimes meant killing Indians. I know the Colonel respected the Sioux—he said so. But he also said it didn't matter what we thought of the Indians because our duty was to make the land safe for settlers. Still, you could tell he didn't like having to kill Indians all the same.

Once, after he shot this sorta famous Sioux

name of Black Wolf, he got all quiet and serious
for a while—stayed in his tent for a coupla days, in
fact. Me, I hated the Indian fighting on account of
I just couldn't stand the thought of getting
scalped. After finding a man without his scalp, you
kinda couldn't help picturing yourself laying there
like that one day. And it's funny, but I developed
this habit of reaching up to feel if my hair was still
there after a battle, as if they coulda taken it somehow without my knowing. Even today, if I get star-
tled by a loud noise or something, the old hand
sneaks on up to my scalp quick as a wink. Makes
me laugh now, 'cause there ain't enough hair left
up there for an Indian to grab ahold of.

Anyway, when that round of fighting was
over, once again us soldiers without kin to speak
of had to figure out where we was headed. Oh,
we kidded the married fellers about how they
had to quit putting off the inevitable now and go
home to resume the war with the missus, that
kinda nonsense. But the truth is, there warn't one
of us bachelors who hadn't already figured out
that being alone at the end of the day warn't all it
was cracked up to be, and I guess we all secretly
envied those family men. Well, Colonel
Braddock was an observant type, to say the least,
and kindhearted on top. He walked over to
where us loners was sorta moping around and
says he's got a proposition for anyone who's interested.

"What'd you have in mind, Colonel?" says
Dobbs.

"Well," says Abel, "I just got word my father passed away, so I've got to go back to Texas to take over the family ranch. But the fact is, Pa never had enough help around the place, so I was wondering if any of you boys wanted to tag along. It's hard work, all right, but the pay's good—I'll see to that. Interested?"

To be honest, none of us really wanted to ride a thousand miles to go herding cattle. But because it was Abel who was asking, it seemed like the smart thing to do. That's the effect he had on a person. Besides, none of us was about to turn him down. We each owed the man our lives a dozen times over, and now here he was again, playing the good samaritan and all. I reckon even if a beautiful woman had come along at that moment and invited me to go prospecting for gold with her instead, I would've had to say no.

And so, after saying good-bye to the boys at Fort Abercrombie—Yankees, every last one of 'em, but good men—and buying ourselves some really fine horses with our back pay, the six of us hit the trail and headed south. We made it most of the way, having crossed through Indian territory without seeing a one, and was a good hundred miles into Texas proper when Johnny, who admitted to having a smidgen of Indian blood in him, said it felt like we was being followed. Abel said he thought we should tie up behind some trees up ahead and wait for whoever it was. He said he wanted to know what we thought. Well, we may not have been calling him "Colonel" no more, but it was gonna take a hell of a lot longer for us to stop treating him like one. We all just sorta stood there, looking down at our feet, and Abel guessed what was up.

"All right," he says, pretending to be angry. "Just this one last time I'll let you all be soldiers instead of men who actually have brains to think with, but from now on I expect you all to have something to say in these situations."

Anyhow, we all done like he said and tied up and waited. Sure enough, ten, fifteen minutes later, along comes this seedy looking character, and when he sees us he tries to bolt. But Abel just shoots the horse out from under him, and we soon had him talking. Said his name was Tommy Maha and that he worked for Abel's uncle, Red Braddock. Abel, who never flinched, sorta stiffened a little when he heard this.

"What do you mean, you *work* for him?" Abel asked him, eyeing the man like he was the plague.

"He sent me to kill you, Mr. Braddock," says Maha, who talked like he was being choked or something and looked like a rat wearing a hat that was too big. Well, now we was *all* giving him the evil eye, but *good*. And in those days, we were a pretty ornery looking bunch, if I do say so myself.

"Are you throwing yourself on our mercy?" asked Dobbs like he couldn't believe what he was hearing.

"Not at all, gentlemen," says Maha, cool as

you please. "Actually, I came here to warn you, Mr. Braddock. Here." He handed Abel a letter from Abel's uncle addressed to Maha. It said he would get five-hundred dollars to kill Abel.

I never saw it before or since, but Abel went all white for a second. Then, just like that, he was his old self again.

"But why were you so far behind us," he asked, "and why the hell did you make me shoot your damn horse if you're here to warn me?"

"I was trying to catch up with you, but my horse was lame," says Maha. "And I didn't expect so many men would be riding with you. When I came around those trees, I thought *I* was being ambushed, so I took off." We checked the man's horse, and it was a bit coon-footed at that. But we didn't let up staring at him. "I see," says Abel. "So I suppose you want me to double the money Red was paying you."

"Oh, no, Mr. Braddock. I don't want your money that way. I want to *work* for you."

The rest of us kinda snickered at that, excepting Johnny, who leaned over and whispered to me that he hoped there'd still be enough jobs for everyone by the time we got to Texas.

Abel was studying the man's face real carefully, though why I don't know, since it was obvious Maha was lying through his pointed, yellow teeth.

"All right, Tommy, you're working for me," Abel says finally, smiling. He was just playing along, of course.

"I want you to go back to Gonzago and tell Red you couldn't find me, then just wait till you hear from me or one of my friends here. Boyd, give him your horse, you ride with Lem."

So off went the little rat on the best horse I ever rode, grinning from ear to ear like he'd fooled us all.

"Abel, I sure hope you know what you're doing," warned Bill. "That man's gonna stick a knife in someone's back before long. I just know it. And why's your own uncle after your hide, if you don't mind my asking?" We were all wondering that. Excepting Indian warriors and Yankee soldiers, we'd never met anyone before who didn't like Abel, let alone someone who wanted him dead—and kinfolk, no less.

"Boys," said Abel, looking up at the darkening sky, "let's set up camp, and over dinner I'll tell you all about the Braddock clan. I suppose you ought to know what you're getting yourselves into."

So we tied up and built a fire, and listened to Abel tell us about his family. And that's where the real story begins.

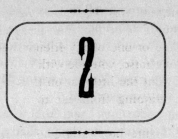

I only wish Abel was here to tell it himself, because I don't remember all the details, but the main idea was that Abel's father was a no-good sonofabitch who just happened to become rich and powerful on account of he was a smart businessman. He started with a few head of second-rate cattle and turned 'em into a ten thousand head ranch. And you won't believe this, but the bastard never let Abel speak a single word to him. He could talk to his mother all he wanted, but not while Abel Sr. was around—that was the rule.

Then, when Abel's mother died, the old man made Abel move out of the big house and into an old toolshed way out on the property somewhere so he didn't have to look at him. Abel had to take his meals with the help after his father left the house. Sounds like a real piece of work, don't he?

Anyway, his brother, Red—his real name was Theodore or something—was always friendly to Abel as a kid, and Abel's father always tried to humiliate Red in front of everyone, so naturally Abel grew up liking Red and hating Abel Sr., and that's the way things stayed.

"So you see, men," said Abel when he'd finished, "I'm inclined to doubt that man's story about his working for Red."

"Then who do you reckon did put him up to it, Abel?" asked Lem.

"Well, I left out one little detail from my past," says Abel like he was tired of thinking about whatever it was. "Before I left town, a man named Quinn Eckhardt drew on me, and I killed him. In those days I couldn't hit air, but he was slower than that fat Yankee sergeant, remember? The one who couldn't reload? Anyway, I just got off a lucky hip shot in his direction and it killed him. The reason he wanted me dead was that I was seeing his daughter, Daphne, at the time, and he didn't like it because he and my father were good friends. The story I heard from Red was that Pa and Quinn both went off to fight in the Mexican war and they both deserted together as soon as the shooting started."

We all went quiet for a minute, just sorta staring into the fire. I was thinking Abel musta felt real good every time he done something brave in the army, which was all the time, 'cause his old man was so yeller, and that it musta really pissed his father off when he heard about Abel becoming a colonel so fast and winning all them medals.

Finally, after a coupla minutes, Dobbs blurts out, "So how'd Daphne take all this?"

"Couldn't tell you," says Abel without even looking up. "I never saw her again after that. I reckon she got over me real quick when she heard about her father. Anyway, she's got a brother, Randy, who I know for certain wants me dead. I figure Randy's trying to be clever by sending Maha out here with a fake letter and a phony story. Too bad he didn't send someone more believable—as if I'd go running back to Elsinore and kill Red on the basis of what that little weasel had to say!"

"So how are you going to handle this Randy character?" asked Dobbs.

"Oh, I'll deal with him later. Anyone that stupid can wait. But keep your eyes open anyway. Randy's the type who'd sooner shoot you in the back while you're sleeping than challenge you to a fair fight."

Abel didn't say another word. He just lay down and looked up at the stars for a while. Now, none of us said anything, but we was all thinking that there was even more going on in this Elsinore place we was headed to than what Abel said. It's not that we thought he was lying—that wasn't his way. But, hell, Abel hadn't set foot there in years, and things have a way of changing awful fast while a man's away. And, friend, I don't have to tell you that where there's money, there's bound to be some shady dealings nearby. But being soldiers bred to danger, there warn't one of us layin' there as the fire died out thinking anything but what a relief it was to know we would be saved from the dull life of a working a ranch by the appearance of our old friend trouble.

Like I suspected, when we arrived in Gonzago, Abel didn't recognize the place. Some trail towns just get bigger and bigger while others just sorta never make it. Gonzago was of the first kind, and Abel couldn't help staring around as we sauntered through the place. 'Course, it was no city—you could ride clear through it in a few seconds at a good pace—but you could tell it warn't the dusty little hitching post Abel had left behind before the war.

"Abel," says Lem in a low voice. "Looks like Randy laid out the red carpet for us."

"Yeah, I see 'em," says Abel without so much as a nod. "Just keep riding."

Well, I had no idea what they was going on about, and I was just about to ask when I caught a movement from one of the second-floor windows just ahead of us to the right. Then another, and another. We was being watched, all right, and that probably also meant we had a dozen rifles trained on us, too. All that moving around, though—hell, I thought, looks like this Randy hired some real greenhorns.

"Well, now, if it ain't Abel Braggart, the war hero. If you're looking for a statue of yourself, forget it. Folks around here didn't take it kindly, you going to work for the Union army after the war."

The voice belonged to a scowling, red-faced feller who was leaning in the doorway of a saloon we was passing. We all stopped dead in our tracks when he spoke. Then Abel, who looked all serious at first, let out the hardest laugh I ever heard him give. The scowling feller kinda stiffened at this, and his beady eyes got even narrower, like two slits. Abel senses we was all getting ready to draw, so he puts up his hand ever so slightly, which was the signal for hold your fire. Then he dismounted and tied up at the trough in front of the saloon. We all did likewise and stood around Abel, waiting for his next move. He walked right up to the feller and stood there smiling about a foot away from his nasty red face.

"Randy, don't take this the wrong way," says Abel, "but you look like hell. Still, you do remind me of my childhood, so in a way it's good to see you."

Randy backed off a little. You could tell he was trying to hide how scared he was.

"Hey, Mr. Braddock," says this beefy feller with a long beard who was standing a few feet away. "You prob'ly don't remember me—name's McCullock—but I just want you to know that's bullshit, what Randy there just said about folks in Gonzago. We know you ain't no Yankee lover. We're real proud of what you done in the war, and ain't nobody around here who ever questioned you going off to fight hostiles up in the

Dakota territory. I got some relatives up that way myself, and I'm sure they was plenty grateful to have you and your men around to protect them."

"Thanks—Jimbo, right? Jimbo McCullock. See? I remember," says Abel, shaking the man's big ol' hand. "And call me Abel from now on." The big feller smiled.

"Good to have you back," McCullock says, smiling and nodding to the rest of us. Randy gives him a dirty look, I guess for spoiling his story, but Jimbo just stares him down. Then Abel turns back to Randy.

"I wouldn't try anything, Braddock," says Randy with a sorry quiver in his high-pitched girl's voice. "See, I'm not going to be as easy to get rid of as my pa. And you just stay the hell away from my sister. Otherwise—" Then he makes like he's gonna whistle with his fingers, but Abel stops him.

"Save your breath," says Abel. "Even my blind grandmother couldn't miss that bunch of fidgety amateurs you've got stationed in every second-floor room in town." Then Abel walks out into the middle of the street and in a real loud voice, so that everyone in town could hear, proceeds to give a speech that went something like this: "All right, listen up all you men working for Randy here. I don't know what you're being paid, but it can't be worth getting killed over. Me and my friends here have had a long ride and we're tired, only not so tired that we can't defend ourselves. Those of you who want to wake up tomorrow morning for sure, come on down here now and give back the money Randy paid you. I'll call any man my friend who has the guts to do that. Those of you too proud or stupid to come down, all I can say is you've been warned. You got five minutes."

Well, they didn't need no five minutes to make up their minds. Every last one of 'em came on down just as fast as their legs could carry 'em. You shoulda seen 'em all walk up to Eckhardt and drop the money at his feet. It was like they was worried that putting it in his hand would seem too friendly. Then they all kinda stood there looking down at the ground until Abel starts going around shaking hands with them, and after that you knew Abel would never have to worry about any of that group again.

Now, you can't really blame those men for jumping ship like they did. Remember, it was Abel doing the talking, and, like I said a ways back, the man could talk his way out of a snake bite. It wasn't so much what he said as the way he said it. It's hard to describe to someone who never had dealings with Abel face to face, but it was like he was in charge in whatever situation he happened to be. He knew it and you knew it, and so everything that he said was like gospel out the mouth of a preacher on Sunday. Mind you, I ain't never actually set foot inside a church. I just couldn't seem to get religion myself—excepting, of course, the kind a man gets when he's being shot at and figures his time's up, but I reckon that don't count. Still, I've known enough good Christian folks to have an idea how people get when the spirit moves 'em, and that's how it was when you'd been spoke to kindly by Abel.

'Course, there's always a catch when a man's got it good. Take Abel's ability to talk his way outta things, for instance. One minute he's got fifteen hired killers pointing their guns at him, the next he's stuck with fifteen unemployed men who all want to be his friend. And so, despite the fact that every last one of 'em was probably just as cowardly and desperate as he looked, we all had a drink together to get 'em off Abel's back. I was none too pleased to be socializing with the likes of 'em, but I played along, unlike Bill Evans, who had a look on his face the whole time like he just ate a bad egg.

On our way out, just as we're passing Randy, who was drinking at the other end of the bar with his pile of money in front of him, Abel stops and says to him, real angry all of a sudden, "Just stay out of my way and you might live long enough to kill yourself with whiskey. 'Scuse me."

With that, Abel just brushes past Randy and out of the saloon, leaving him sitting there with his mouth half open and his face redder than ever. The rest of us filed on out behind Abel, tipping our hats to Randy as we passed. He was fit to be tied, all right. But the thing is, none of us ever heard Abel get mad enough to insult a man before, and while it was sorta refreshing to see him lose his temper for once, it was worrisome all the same. I couldn't help thinking that maybe coming back to Gonzago warn't such a good idea after all. Randy was gonna force a showdown, and judging from the color of his face, it'd be sooner than later. Still, as long as he kept hiring quantity instead of quality, we figured that, between our guns and Abel's smooth talking, we could handle things.

Now, as soon as a man starts letting his guard down like that, the world throws everything it's got at him just to teach him a lesson. So after we left and had got about a mile out of town on our way to the ranch, we were coming up out of a gully when all of a sudden the air around us started buzzing with lead. We took up positions in a wink, but that first volley got Dobbs and Massey. We got ten of them, and another ten or so rode off. Fortunately, Dobbs and Massey warn't hurt real bad. The slug that got Lem went clean through the side of his neck, so it was just a matter of stopping the bleeding and cleaning out the wound. Dobbsy, on the other hand, needed a doctor on account of the bullet was still in his shoulder.

"I must be some kind of goddamned magnet or something," says Dobbs. It was true. If there was any wounded in our group after a fight, Dobbsy was always one of them. He used to say he was gonna die of lead poisoning.

After making sure Dobbs and Massey was all right, Abel starts looking over the bodies of the fellers we shot.

"Well," he says, "This here's Billy Phipps—that makes it Randy, all right. Phipps was working for Randy's father before I was even born. And this one over here was a cowhand at Eckhardt's ranch, too, only I don't recall the name. And look—our old friend Tommy Maha."

Soon as I heard the name, I run over to where the dead men's horses were still tied up, thinking for sure I'd find the palomino beauty Maha rode off on, but no such luck.

"Hey, Abel!" shouts Bill from behind a tree nearby, "Take a look at this!"

We all run over to where Bill was standing, and what do we see laying there, stone-cold dead with a bullet through the chest, but a big ol' Comanche.

"If that don't beat all," says I.

"I *knew* I saw an Indian," says Johnny, "I knew it!" He just loved being right, 'cause it almost never happened.

Now, it didn't make sense that a Comanche would hire out to a white man. They traded with the whites all right, in fact, they was regular trading fools. But in them days there was still bands of 'em running wild all over Texas, even with a treaty and the army around. And you'd really have to scrape the barrel to find a plains Indian of any stripe who'd deal with a no-account like Randy Eckhardt. You could see from the look on Abel's face that the same thought was troubling him.

"Must be some sort of outcast or something,"

says Abel finally and walks back over to his horse. It wasn't like Abel to just shrug off a mystery that way, and me and Bill looked at each other without saying a word, but both of us thinking we was maybe headed for more trouble than our Army Colts could get us out of this time.

Then Bill leans down and pulls a little parfleche pouch offa the Comanche's belt. He opens it up and inside he finds a gold coin, only it warn't like no gold piece we ever seen before. It had a sorta cross on it and some words we couldn't make out on account of they was almost rubbed off. We showed it to Abel, who got all interested again. He brings it over to Dobbsy and asks him if he knew what it was.

"Hmm," says Dobbsy. "I can't read what it says, but it's Spanish all right, and quite old."

"You mean Spanish as in Mexican?" asks Abel.

"No," says Dobbsy. "I mean as in Spain. And I could be wrong, but I'd say it's at least a couple hundred years old."

"Any idea how a Comanche might get ahold of something like this?" Abel asks.

"Sorry, Abel," says Dobbsy, a little disappointed that he didn't have all the answers, "but your guess is as good as mine. I'm not sure how anyone would get ahold of one of these outside of a museum."

So Abel puts the coin back in the pouch and tells me to hold on to it real careful. I guess he felt bad about giving my horse to Maha, or maybe knowing about my dream of being a gold prospector, he figured I'd get a kick outta the thing. Either way, I was glad to have it. Then he walks over to his horse looking real worried. Randy hiring notchers to plug us was one thing, but that there Comanche really complicated things.

We left the bodies where they was, but we took the horses, and finally got to the house at Elsinore, which looked like a mansion-sized brothel, if you ask me.

Standing out front to greet us was a man you knew had to be Red on account of his hair. He was about the same height as Abel, but that was as far as the family resemblance went. He had them freckles that all red-headed folk seemed to get, and blue eyes that looked kinda watered down, if you know what I mean.

Well, Red seemed like a nice enough feller, and he got all riled up when he heared about us getting ambushed. He asks us who we thought mighta done it, but just then a serious looking feller with a black bag shows up at the door. Turns out to be Red's doctor, who lived right on the ranch. One of the hands musta sent for him when he saw us ride up with our wounded. The doctor had Lem and Dobbs brought into another room to work on 'em, and then Red and Abel started talking over old times for a while. So me and Evans decided to take a look around the place.

Right away, I knew that something was

wrong when I recognized a feller who deserted the unit at Stones River. I mean, it was a working ranch and all, and most of the hands looked like they belonged. But here and there you'd see a dark, stringy looking feller with those eyes a man gets when he's got a price on his head.

"Boyd," says Bill to me kinda under his breath as we rode around. "I know the man is the only kin Abel's got left, but Red is either blind or up to no good. This here farm is crawling with horse thieves, and worse. See that one there, with the scar across his forehead?"

The man he was pointing at was just about the meanest-looking cuss I'd ever laid eyes on. When he sees me, he tries to smile, only it comes out upside down.

"That there's Jerome Sykes. Last time I saw him he was doing life in prison. Wonder how he got out? And there's a couple more familiar faces around. Looks like Red's got some explaining to do."

3

When we got back to the house and had a chance to talk to Abel alone, we told him about Sykes and the rest, and he just goes right up to Red and asks him about it.

"My friends here," says Abel, "are concerned that maybe you weren't aware some of your men around here are outlaws."

"Gentlemen," says Red, looking at me and Bill with a big, warm smile. "I make a deal with all my help when I hire them. I don't ask about a man's background, and he works his damned ass off for me. I'm trying to run the biggest ranch probably in the whole world, so I demand a lot from my men. If they give me what I want here, I don't give a damn who they were in the outside world. Oh, I know there's a few scoundrels in the bunch, but they don't cause any trouble once they're here."

Well, Abel seemed satisfied with the explanation, and that was good enough for us, though I
was thinking a man oughta be more careful who
he hires, especially out here, where there's hardly
any law around. One look at that Sykes feller 'n
you'd be thinking the same thing.

Over supper that night, Lem and Dobbsy
rejoined the group, and after 'bout an hour of
small talk, Abel finally puts it to Red about how
we was all gonna fit in around Elsinore.

"So anyway, Red," says Abel, "I guess you
know why I've come back."

"Why sure, Abe," says Red all smiling-like.
"You want to work the ranch, right?"

"Well, yeah, Red, I thought I would. But not
at your expense, old friend. I mean, you'll stay on
and be my supervisor, and whatever your take of
the profits is, that won't change. And until I can
learn from watching you, which'll take a while,
you'll still be in charge of things."

Well, if he was hiding anything, he sure was
doing a good job of it, 'cause Red looked and
sounded all relieved, like he'd just been waiting
for the chance to turn Elsinore over to someone
who wanted the damn place.

"I'm telling you, Abe," he says, getting up
and slapping Abel on the back. "It's going to be
great—just like old times, only without—" Then
he stops suddenly, looking me and Bill over.

"It's all right, Red, they know all about Pa,"
says Abel.

"Well," Red went on, "I'm sure there's

nothing I can teach you about being in charge that the army didn't already make you learn in spades. As for all the little details of running a big ranch, I reckon you'll be a natural once you get the hang of it. But to be honest with you, I'm worried you'll be bored stiff after a few weeks, what with fighting Yankees and Indians for the last seven years."

"Oh, we got used to boredom long ago, didn't we boys?" says Abel with a grin.

We all nodded and mumbled real convincingly that we surely did. Fighting Indians was dangerous and all, but, like I said, in between fights was a whole lotta nothing.

Then Red asks again if we knowed who tried to drygulch us, and so Abel tells Red about what happened to us in town. Red laughed real hard when he hears how Abel talked all those men into giving Randy back his money. But when Abel finished, Red got all serious. He walks over to the window and stands there, looking out for a minute without saying a word.

"Randy," he says finally, shaking his head, "Yeah, we're gonna have to figure something out there."

"Oh, don't fret over him," says Abel. "From now on I'll be two steps ahead of his little traps. Me and my friends here can handle him."

"You don't understand," says Red, rubbing his eyes. "See, Randy works for me."

Well, you shoulda seen the look on Abel's face when he heard that. I guess he probably looked something like me, Dobbsy, Bill, and Lem did. But now, don't go feeling sorry for Johnny on account of how I left him out—the look on Johnny's face never changed, whether he was staring off into space or wrestling a Sioux warrior to death. If he'd 'a wanted, he coulda made a fortune playing poker with that face of his, but he just didn't care for card games.

Anyway, so Abel asks Red what he meant.

"Well," says Red, "It's just that I promised Daphne I'd keep Randy out of trouble, and the only way I know how is to keep him working."

"Today must've been his day off," says Dobbs before we could shush him up, but Abel didn't hear. Now *he* was on his feet looking out that window.

"So tell me," says Abel after taking in the view for a spell, "how *is* Daphne? I mean, how'd she take it when she heard about me and Quinn?"

"Actually," says Red, "Daphne and me never even said how'dya do until a year or so after you left town. Your father bought the Eckhardt ranch from her and Randy, and he put me in charge of rebranding all their cattle, and I'd sleep in the Eckhardt house because I didn't feel like riding there and back every day. I was also supposed to evict Randy and Daphne from the house, but I never could get up the nerve. I s'pose if it'd just been Randy I'd have managed, but with Daphne, well, *you* ought to know.

"So I let them stay and I never told your

father, and he was too busy with other business to bother checking. I guess Daphne was grateful, and we've been friends ever since. We never did discuss the shoot-out between you and Quinn, but judging from the way Daphne still talks kindly about you, I'd say she probably blamed her father for what happened, like everyone else in these parts. But she's coming by in a few days, so you can ask her yourself."

"Oh," says Abel, clearing his throat. "Is she?"

Now this here's a good example of the way a woman gets under a man's skin so's he can't think of nothing else. One minute the conversation's about a feller who's trying to kill Abel with every gun for hire in Texas, and the next minute all Abel cares about is some girl he used to hold hands with when he was a schoolboy. But, to be fair to Abel, I will say that this Daphne was what Dobbsy would call a goddess, the kinda woman you never forgot no matter how many women you had after her. She was so beautiful that even folks who knew her since she was a child had to sneak a stare at her when she walked by. After getting a look at her brother, it didn't seem possible that they coulda come from the same family, but that's the way it works sometimes.

"You know," says Red, "I think what I'll do is have Randy run a small herd up to Abilene tomorrow—that'll keep him out of your hair for a while. And while he's gone, I'll try to figure out something a little more permanent."

"Red, if you know Randy," says Abel, "you know how he feels about me. The only permanent solution that's gonna work short of me plugging the damn fool is for one of us to leave town for good, and I just got here."

"I know," says Red. "In a way I wish he'd given you the excuse to gun him down when you first arrived. Would've saved us all a lot of trouble. But we gotta consider Daphne, too. She can't be blamed for caring about the little weasel. He's her brother, after all, and I'm sure you don't want to see her get hurt any more than I do. She might've forgiven you for killing her father, but I wouldn't push it. So let me at least try to come up with a way to salvage this mess."

"All right," says Abel, "for Daphne's sake, go ahead and try. Just don't be surprised if it all blows up in your face. Randy's got a one-track mind now that I'm back in town, and he's gonna see through any of your schemes to keep us apart." Red kinda frowned and nodded.

"I got to at least try," he says.

Abel just stands there for a bit, and Red finally says we all must be dead tired, which was true enough, especially Lem and Dobbsy. Red had his maid put clean sheets on some of the spare beds in the house, and we all turned in, and I ain't exaggerating when I tell you I had the best night's sleep since before I joined the army.

Well, after a coupla days of being a cowhand, I decided I'd rather go back up north and take on the entire Sioux nation singlehanded. Lem and

Bill was of my mind on that point, but Johnny just dove on into his new line of work right away, bulldogging steers like they was nothing at all. In fact, the first one he got ahold of he dragged down so hard he broke the poor critter's neck— honest to God. 'Course, the first one *I* tried to land almost broke *my* neck, so they made me a flanker instead, which meant holding on to the legs of calves while they was getting branded so they wouldn't kick. I also wound up fixing a lot of fences.

Meanwhile, Dobbsy was gonna be laid up for a week or so till his wound healed, and I suddenly found myself cursing my luck that it warn't me who took a bullet in the shoulder. I reckon the thing I hated most about the work itself was the smell. I'd never really thought about it before, but that many head of cattle make an awful lot of manure. Now, I can't honestly say it was as bad as the smell of being downwind of a battlefield before all the bodies got buried, but it sure was close, especially in the afternoon, when the Texas sun really got things heated up. But there was something even worse than the work.

See, none of us ever figured we'd have any boss but Abel once we got to Elsinore. But Abel was off with Red—you know, learning the ropes as they say—and until Abel knew how to run things, the rest of us had to answer to one of Red's men, which turned out to be none other than that Sykes feller. He tells us the first day that he knowed we was friends of Red's nephew and all, but that he was gonna have to work us just as hard as any other hand around, 'cause if he gave us special treatment then everyone would want it.

"That's all right," says Lem. "We never got special treatment when we was in the army, and we don't want any from you. We come here to work."

Well, that was a big mistake. As soon as Lem opened his yap, Sykes got all narrow-eyed, and you could tell he was glad to have the opportunity to hit back.

"Oh, yeah, Red told me you was soldiers. Well, soldier, you're gonna wish you stayed in the army by the time I'm finished with ya. And that goes for yer friends there, too."

Now, Bill didn't look up from what he was doing this whole time until Sykes started threatening us.

"Lookee here, cowboy," says Bill as he stood up. "There's no need to get all up on your hind legs like that. We don't mind an honest day's work, but we didn't come all the way here from the Dakotas to be pushed around by anyone, least of all by the likes of you."

Suddenly, Sykes was off his horse and standing chin to chin with Bill.

"Whaddya mean, the likes of me?" he says with his hand sorta twitching in the air above his holster.

"C'mon, Bill," I says, tryin' to keep things from getting any hotter. "Let's not wear out our welcome the first day." I hated to have to pussy-foot around like that, but you could see right off that Sykes was the kind of feller who would never back down once he was provoked. I was damned if we was gonna start something, at least before Abel give us the word. But it was too late.

"Go on, soldier boy," says Sykes as he backed up just far enough to get a clear draw, "finish what you was about to say."

"Aw, forget it," says Bill, trying his damndest to do right by Abel.

"Just like I figured," says Sykes, who showed no signs of cooling off. "You army types are all yeller when it comes to a fair fight, man to man."

Then, all of a sudden, he recognizes Bill.

"Say, now, just a damn minute," he says, eyeing Bill with his ugly, upside-down smile. "I seen you in the hoosegow. Well, well, ain't that something. I thought I saw that godawful face of yers somewhere before."

"Took you long enough, shit for brains," says Bill, who I reckon just couldn't stand it no more. Sykes's face turned red, and he went to draw. But before he gets his gun all the way outta the holster, a rock smacks Sykes square in the forehead, and he falls over backward and winds up flat on his back, out cold.

We all turn around in the direction it come from and see Johnny standing there about twenty feet off, dusting off his hands. He mighta been dumber than that rock he threw, but like I said before, Johnny was a good man to have around in a scrape. He coulda shot Sykes easy enough, and so could the rest of us, but Johnny always seemed to know when to use his gun and when not to. Once, when we was lying in wait for a pair of Union scouts to go by ahead of their main force, one of 'em sees us. In the split second before they can sound the alarm, Johnny just leaps up from his hiding place and bashes their two heads together, knocking them out. The rest of us were gonna just shoot 'em, which, of course, would've brought all the other Yankees down on top of us in a flash. It was as if the good Lord, seeing he forgot to give Johnny a regular portion of smarts, decided to make up for it by giving him an extra helping of what they call instinct.

"Nice work, Johnny," says Lem as he checked to see if Sykes was still breathing. But Johnny didn't answer. He was already back at work like nothing happened.

So we disarmed Sykes, told Johnny to keep an eye on him, and walked back to the house, hoping to find Abel and Red. They were out front talkin' when we got there, and we told them about Sykes.

"Damn that Sykes," says Red. "And just after I got through telling you all how well behaved my men are. Well, you won't have to worry about him anymore. Slim!"

Just then a tall and skinny feller comes running up from behind the house. Red, who looked good and mad, said, Excuse me, and walked off with the man he called Slim toward where we left Sykes, talking in low voices.

"Boys," says Abel, "I'm real proud of the way you handled that. But, hell, don't feel you can't defend yourselves on my account. If you have to shoot, you go right ahead."

"Abel," says Lem. "You just keep Johnny nearby with a good supply of rocks."

We were all having a good laugh about that when two shots rang out from the direction where we left Johnny and Sykes. We all run back, guns drawn, and when we get there we find the feller Red called Slim dragging Sykes away with a hole in his temple and Red standing there holding a gun. Johnny come up and told us that Red just walked up and shot Sykes without saying a word. Red holsters his gun and walks on over.

"I'm sorry you boys had to see all this, but I had to lay down the law. Believe me, there won't be any more trouble around *this* ranch for a while."

"Jesus, Red," says Abel, kinda stunned. "You can't just drop a man like that in cold blood."

"Cold blood nothing!" says Red. "I know Sykes—soon as his head cleared he would have made it his business to kill some or all of your men. I don't blame them for standing up to him. Hell, I wouldn't have let him ride me, either, and I'm just an old rancher."

We all just stood there looking Red straight in the eye.

"You're probably thinking I'm a fool for

allowing desperadoes like him to work for me in the first place," he says, throwing his gun down in disgust. "And you know what? I'm beginning to think you're right."

Without saying another word, Red walks slowly back toward the house, leaving us standing there wondering what's next.

4

Now like I told you before, Abel Sr. was a hero, almost a legend, in this part of Texas. The locals talked about him the way people back east talk about President Lincoln, or the way my uncle Malcolm used go on about all them famous Scottish kings. He was everyone's hero in Gonzago 'cause, if it hadn't been for Abel Braddock Sr., the whole area woulda just been wide-open land for the Comanche and Kiowa to run around on. And, you know, I reckon even if everyone in Texas did know what a skunk the man was, it wouldn'ta made no difference. That's on account of how money and power work like liquor on the minds of folks who ain't got any.

All anybody in Gonzago knew was that Abel Sr. was a real smart business man who made the town what it was, and that was that. And I reckon they can't be blamed for being a mite resentful of

Red when he took over after his brother died. Everyone knew Red never amounted to much on his own, so they figured he oughtn't be allowed to just come walking in and replace Abel Sr. the way he did.

And then the rumors started up about Abel's death being kinda mysterious, now that everyone thought about it, and how Red's friend Dr. Peters was in charge of looking after Abel Sr. while he was sick, and how nobody but Red ever saw the body before they buried it, and so on. So by the time we all rode into town, folks were so worked up about it all that there was talk of lynching Red. 'Course, we didn't know about this when we arrived.

Well, we found out, all right. After Red walked off, Abel decides he wants to go back into town to look up old friends. And besides, Daphne wouldn't be around till the next day. So we took our pick of horses from the stable and saddled up. The one I got warn't half the horse I gave that Maha feller, and I let everyone know about it all the way back to Gonzago.

It was a lot busier in town that evening than when we first showed up. There was people everywhere you looked, and the sound of an old piano and drunken singing filled the air. The sunset was the color of fire, and all in all it seemed like a good night to sample the pleasures of our new home. The occasional gun shot gave it just the right touch. Abel says we should just go and have a good time and he'd catch up with us later, after he done some calling. So me, Lem, Johnny and Dobbs ended up back in the same saloon we was in the first day—it was called Wilson's Tavern—and after a coupla whiskeys, everything was all right.

Well, we're sitting at a table off in a corner, laughing at some joke Lem was telling, and all of a sudden I notice everyone in the whole place is just kinda staring at us. I turned back to hear the story out, but outta the corner of my eye I see they're not just staring; they're whispering and pointing, like we was dressed funny or something. Then, I notice the bartender ain't all that friendly, kinda slamming the bottle down on our table and so on.

"You know," I says to the others, "I'm getting the feeling that folks around here don't think so highly of us."

"Yeah," says Dobbsy. "Now that you mention it, we do seem to be getting some dirty looks at that."

"What do you reckon it is?" asks Lem.

"I don't know, Lem," says Dobbsy getting to his feet, "but I'll be damned if I'm going to sit here getting stared at all night." Then Dobbsy stands up, a little wobbly on account of all the drink.

"Excuse me," he says real loud. "May I have your attention, please."

Oh, brother, I thought, this oughta be good. Dobbsy had everyone's attention, all right. Whatever bee was in their bonnets, the crowd at

Wilson's seemed relieved that Dobbs went and got things started for them, 'cause they gathered around us in a hurry like we was giving money away, only they looked kinda mad. Then Dobbsy spoke up again.

"If anyone here has a problem with me and my friends, now's the time to get it off your chest. C'mon, don't be shy. You there, with the hat on backwards. What's on your mind?"

The feller Dobbsy was talking to got a little embarrassed by the remark about his hat, which did kinda look like it was the wrong way around, and some of his friends musta thought so too, 'cause they couldn't help laughing.

"Will you shut the hell up?" he says, turning to his friends. "Whose side are you on, anyway?" Then he turns back to Dobbsy.

"First of all, it ain't on backwards—it's the latest style and you'll all be wearing one before long. And second, what we got to say needs to be said to Abel Braddock himself." The rest of the crowd mumbled in agreement.

"Abel's tied up at the moment," answers Dobbsy, "but I think I speak for my friends here when I tell you that I got to know right now just what in hell is up your noses."

The feller with the funny hat looked around the room for a minute, until a coupla the others nodded to him to go ahead.

"Well," he says, "it's like this. The whole town's got a lot of respect for Colonel Braddock, and it ain't really anyone's place to go telling him what he ought to do. But we thought he come home to settle the score with Red, not move in with him and his band of rustlers."

"Settle the score?" says Lem. "What do you mean?"

And so they tell us about how everyone thinks Red had Abel Sr. poisoned or something and how the whole town of Gonzago was about ready to string up Red from the nearest tree, only they can't on account of all the protection Red hired.

"I see," says Dobbsy, knowing we couldn't say nothing about what an asshole Abel Sr. was and all. "So let me get this straight. On the one hand, you say it's not your place to tell the Colonel what to do, but on the other hand if he doesn't do what you want him to you're ready to run him out of town? Well, I'd like to see you try."

"Now, just a minute, mister," says one of the men in the crowd. "Who said anything about running anybody out of town? We only wanted to talk the matter over with Colonel Braddock. We were just concerned for his safety, is all."

"That's right," says another feller.

"Oh, is that all?" says Dobbsy, acting all relieved at the news. "I'm sure the Colonel would be touched and all, but don't worry. Do you boys have any idea how many men Colonel Braddock killed in the war? How many Sioux and Cheyenne he personally sent under with his bare hands?" The crowd kinda livened up at this, like a pack of wolves that smelled blood.

"Is it true," asks one feller in the back, "that Colonel Braddock never took no prisoners?"

"Yeah, and did he really take scalps off'n the Injuns he plugged?" asks a toothless old geezer with a gleam in his eye.

"Boys, boys," says Dobbsy, holding up his hands. "I really can't go into all that, not behind the Colonel's back. But I wouldn't put him to the test, if you know what I mean."

Dobbsy sure was laying it on thick, but he had to buy some time till Abel could figure out what he wanted to do about the situation.

"So you can all just relax," says Dobbsy, putting his feet up on the table as if to show everyone just how relaxed they oughta be. "Abel Braddock never backs down from anyone, and once he finds a way to prove Red killed his father, you can be sure honor will be served. Meanwhile, you just let Abel handle it his own way. Besides, Red's not going anywhere, so what's the hurry?"

The men were disappointed they warn't gonna see some action right away, but they owned that Dobbsy had a point there, and so after a few more tall tales, the crowd slowly broke up till there was just the five of us again.

"Nice work, Dobbsy," I says. "I reckon you coulda sold snake oil to that mob." Dobbs was just eating it up.

"Ahem, well," he says, "my daddy *was* a diplomat, after all."

"Yeah, real nice, Dobbs," says Lem, shakin'

his head. "Only you might have at least told 'em that business about Abel taking scalps was horse shit."

Anyway, Abel finally shows up with some friend of his name of Wendel Collins, who leaves after being introduced all around. So then we tell him about what's going on around Gonzago, and he says, yeah, Wendel already told him everything.

"Well, now we know why Red's been hiring outsiders and criminals," says Abel. "No one else will work for him in these parts. Wendel told me that when Pa died, word went out that any man caught working for Red wouldn't be welcome in town."

"This Wendel feller," I says. "Can we trust him?"

"Well, yes and no," says Abel. "He and I grew up together, so I don't think there's anything he wouldn't do for me. But as far as what side he's on with respect to Red, he's the same as everyone else around here. In fact, he said if I needed any help dealing with Red and his boys I should just let him know and he'd have a posse ready to go in less than an hour. Can you believe that?"

"Funny how they couldn't get that posse together all this time, then we show up and they're raring to go. I s'pose everyone in Gonzago's been holding off on killing Red all these months out of courtesy to you, then," says Lem.

"Yeah," added Dobbsy in his usual tone.

"They just didn't want to spoil your fun. Good to be home, huh Abel?"

We all had a good snicker at that. Then Dobbsy asks Abel what we was gonna do next, hoping, like me and Lem was, that ranch work warn't in the plans for a while. Johnny, of course, would be happy either way.

"Well, the more I think about that Comanche," says Abel, "the more it worries me. Eckhardt can be managed as long as all he's got to work with is whatever horse thieves and scum aren't punching cattle for Red over at Elsinore. And anyway I think the message is out that siding with Randy can be bad for the health. But if he starts stirring up trouble with the local Comanches, he could endanger this whole area. I know I shouldn't care what happens to the good people of Gonzago—although I reckon it's not their fault they couldn't see through my father. But according to Wendel, there are a lot of vulnerable homesteaders in these parts, and as it is there are Comanches within a couple hundred miles of here raiding at will lately. Now, they're just small splinter groups, not likely to mass together and pose a real threat the way it stands now. But that could change."

"You mean, whatever Randy's up to might get them on the warpath?" asks Lem.

"I mean," says Abel, "Randy's the kind of selfish bastard who'd stir up every hostile in Texas if he thought it would mess up my plans to settle down here and live on the ranch in peace. And treaty or no treaty, all Comanches love the wild life. If you give them any excuse to go whooping it up like in the good old days, they'll take it. Can't say I blame them there."

"So what'll we do?" asks Dobbs.

"I think we'll pay the local Comanches a little visit," says Abel.

Well, that was more like it, I thought. Back in the saddle and into dangerous Indian territory again. I guess I ain't so diff'rent from those Indians, when you come right down to it.

We rode back out to Elsinore and got some sleep, and the next morning we told Red where we was headed and why.

"Oh, Christ," says Red, "that idiot Randy! Just like him to screw up five years of hard work keeping the locals and the Comanches from trying to wipe each other out." Red was real angry.

"I wish you'd told me before about that warrior," he says. "I'd have gone straight out to their village and talked to them myself. Well, maybe it's not too late—I'll go now."

"Great," says Abel, "we'll keep you company."

"I'd rather you didn't, Abe," says Red, putting his hand on Abel's shoulder. "One man alone will be less likely to get them stirred up. And anyway, I've established a trade relationship with Many Horses, the chief of the local tribe."

Damn it, I thought, there goes our fun.

"All right," says Abel, "if you say so. Oh, and

while you're there, see if you can find out where this came from. We found it on the Comanche." Abel motioned for me to give him the gold piece, and he threw it over to Red.

"A gold piece," says Red without hardly looking at it. "So what? You know how Indians love trinkets. Hell, they hand down those presidential medals from one generation to the next. You know, the ones the government gives them when they sign a treaty?"

"I know," says Abel, "but Dobbs here says it's an old Spanish coin, the kind you'd only find in a museum."

"Yeah?" says Red, giving the coin a good, hard look. "Whadd'ya know about that. Probably took it during a raid, maybe from some fellow who stole it from someplace back east. Who knows? Anyway, that's the only explanation I can think of." Then he throws it back to Abel, who shrugs and throws it back to me. To be honest, I was kinda glad it turned out not to be important 'cause, for a minute, I thought I wasn't gonna get it back.

"While I'm gone," says Red as he strapped on his holster, "you and your men can see my new foreman about what to do. His name's Slim and—oh, here he comes now."

The door opens and in walks the skinny feller we saw the day before. He had a blank look on his face, kinda like Johnny, only not as friendly. Red tells him where he was going and takes off, leaving Slim and us standing there.

"This way, boys," he says, and we follow him outside. He gives us all things to do, except for Dobbsy, who still couldn't hardly move his arm, so he just stayed at the house. Said he was gonna relax and catch up on his reading in Red's library. 'Course, it warn't so much a library as a bunch of old books stacked in a corner, but, like I said, Dobbs was educated and he loved to read. I remember during the war when we took over a house for the night he'd go right for where the books were and take as many as he could stuff in his pack.

Anyhow, Slim put the rest of us to work on one thing or another, Abel, as usual, taking on the toughest and dirtiest jobs for himself. Now, this Slim feller mighta looked kinda seedy, but he spoke like a real gentleman and wasn't lording it over us the way Sykes done. The only thing about him was he had this raspy cough. Couldn't get a sentence out without throwing a coupla coughs in at the end. But I reckon if he coulda helped it he would.

Well, after a full day's work I realized that not only was I beginning to find the chores tolerable, but that I was getting used to the godawful smell, too. Mind you, I still felt like I'd go outta my head if I had to fix corral fence and herd cattle for the rest of my life, but I figured we all owed it to Abel to give it some time. Besides, Abel needed us nearby as long as Randy was still alive, and if Abel could handle shoveling cow shit, so could I.

About sundown, we was headed back to the house for some chow when Red come up behind us on his horse.

"Well, boys," he says, "how's the ranch life suit you so far?"

"It's hard work, but the time passes quickly enough," says Abel. "I assume the fact that you're still alive means that all's well in the Comanche camp."

"Oh, everything's fine," says Red. "Turns out that warrior you killed wasn't even missed."

"How's that possible?" Abel asked.

"Well, you see," says Red, "he was one of those poor devils without any coups, and he was getting a little long in the tooth, so he left the tribe about a year back. Must have gotten tired of not having any say around his own."

"So he hired out to Randy," says Abel with a half smile. "Poor devil is right. That's sinking low even for a white man. I guess when you've got nothing to lose, it's the same in any culture. Call me crazy, but I feel sorry for him ending up that way."

That was Abel, always seeing things from the other feller's point of view. For all he knew, that no-account Comanche had Abel in his sights when he got killed. Now me, I figured he probably had it coming, so good riddance. I'll grant you that being a Plains Indian, especially a warrior, was no picnic, but that's about as far as my sympathy goes. And this *coup* business that Red was talkin' about? In case you never heard of it, coup was how the Indian showed his bravery. It meant he'd touched his enemy during a fight. But, hell, the enemy could be dead already when he touched him, and he could even use a stick, so he didn't even have to get off his horse! To my way of thinking, you really had to wonder about a warrior who couldn't manage even once, in all the battles his tribe fought during his lifetime, to whack a dead body with a stick.

When we got back to the house, I went to find Dobbsy, but he warn't in the so-called library. I looked around outside, I yelled out his name, I asked some of the other hands if they knew where he was, but there was just no sign of him. I told Abel and Red about it, and Red had a coupla his men search the area while we went inside and started supper.

Halfway through eating, one of Red's men came in and said one of the horses was missing from the stable. Well, that settled it. Dobbsy musta gone sightseeing or rode into town or something, so we all relaxed about it.

After dark, we was all sitting around telling Red and Slim some of our best war stories when we heard a stage pull up.

"That'd be Daphne," says Red, and he goes out to meet her. I'd forgotten she was due in. Meanwhile, Abel was on his feet and pacing back and forth like I never seen him do before. Then I noticed for the first time that he went and got all spiffed up for her, and I had to smile at that. Poor feller was still crazy about the girl. I only hoped he warn't in for a disappointment, like maybe she got fat or didn't care for him no more.

Well, soon as she walks in, I could see why she got Abel all worked up. Like I said before, she was beautiful, the kind of pretty you just never saw in places like Gonzago. But she woulda stood out any place on earth, I reckon, and I gotta admit to feeling a tad jealous of Abel at that moment. She had a waist no bigger'n a man's thigh around. Her eyes were sky blue, and her blond, wavy hair went halfway down her back. Anyway, the two of 'em just kinda stood there for a minute, staring at one another like they couldn't believe their own eyes. Then Abel snaps outta his daze and starts introducing everyone.

"Pleased to meet you, ma'am," I says with a sorta half bow. She smiles and nods at me, but then, as Abel turns away toward where Bill and Lem are, by God if she didn't wink at me, like a New Orleans whore trying to get work! As you can imagine, I was so surprised I nearly fell over. The only one to notice anything was Bill, who didn't see the wink, but who musta seen my reaction, 'cause he gave me this look like, "What the hell is your problem, Boyd?"

So we all go into the parlor and had some brandy, which I never tasted before and didn't know you weren't supposed to guzzle down like cheap whiskey, but that's just what I did.

"Easy there, Boyd," says Red. "You're supposed to sip brandy."

"Oh yeah?" I says, draining my glass anyway on account of what just happened with Daphne. "Why's that?"

"Not sure, now that you mention it," says Red. "I guess because it's thirty bucks a bottle!"

Everyone laughed at that except for me and Johnny, who nearly spit out the brandy he had in his mouth when he heard how expensive it was.

"Thirty dollars?" he says, looking like he did that time when Dobbs tried to explain to him that the world wasn't flat. "Lord almighty," he went on. "That's more than my pa made in a whole year! I don't mean no disrespect, Red, but I reckon whoever sold you that bottle pulled a fast one on you."

Well, everyone had a good laugh at that, too. Even I started to chuckle, when suddenly I caught Daphne's eye again, and wouldn't you know she winks at me again! I looked around at everyone, but nobody was paying attention. She sure picked her moments carefully, that woman. Then she turns to Abel and they start holding hands and talking in a low whisper. I decided I'd had enough.

"Excuse me," I said as I stood up. "I think I'll take a walk in the night air. Mighty pleased to make your acquaintance, Miss Eckhardt." I barely looked at her as I said this, but I could see her smiling back at me politely like nothing had happened.

"Yeah," says Bill. "I think I'll join you, Boyd. Ma'am."

I was glad Bill was excusing himself too, 'cause I just had to get this Daphne thing offa my chest. So as soon as we were outside, I told Bill what happened.

"Aw, come on, Boyd," he says, "don't be ridiculous. I think you've been without a woman too long. You're starting to see things."

"Look," I says, "I know it sounds crazy. I mean, I ain't no lady killer or nothing, but I saw what I saw."

Bill could see I was serious, and he knowed I warn't given to telling tales.

"Well," he says, "then I guess Abel oughta know about it."

"Don't be a damn fool!" I says. "You wanna turn Abel against me? You ever seen him so inside out over a woman before?"

"Yeah," he says, scratching his head. "You got that right. So what'll we do?"

"Dunno," I says, "but I sure as hell am gonna stay clear of that hussy. Reckon we oughta tell Lem, though, and Dobbsy when he gets back. Maybe he'll know what to do."

"What about Johnny?" he says. I just looked at him like he was outta his head.

"Sorry," he says. Then we turned in, but I hardly slept at all 'cause I couldn't stop thinking about Daphne. Mainly, I was concerned for what she was gonna do to Abel, but part of me was mulling over how much I woulda liked to have her myself. Ain't that something? There I was, on the one hand knowing she was gonna bring nothing but trouble to a man I owed my life to many times over, and that if I had any sense I oughta get up and go shoot her right then and there. But on the other hand, I was also feeling like I'd do just about anything to get under that dress of hers.

Finally, I went as quiet as I could down the hallway, which was pitch-black, into the parlor, and gulped down some more of that high-end brandy. That musta done the trick, 'cause next thing I knew I was laying on the couch in the parlor with the sun coming in through the window and into my face.

As I sat up, I suddenly noticed Daphne staring down at me. I sorta jumped a little and wound up falling off the couch and whacking my head on the floor. I got up, found my hat, and edged on past her outta the room, never taking my eyes offa her face, which had an evil-looking smile on it. After that, any ideas I had of sleeping with Daphne were gone, and all I could think was she was up to something.

I went outside to clear my head. I seen a figure standing up on a little hill behind the house which turned out to be Johnny, so I walked up there and stood next to him.

Johnny just nods and keeps looking toward the east. I stopped trying to figure out what game Daphne might be playing at and concentrated instead on what pretty country we was in and what a beautiful morning it was. Somewhere overhead you could hear the far-off screech of a hawk or an eagle, and soon a warm breeze blew up.

"So," I says finally. "Some day, ain't it?" But Johnny didn't say nothing. He warn't never one for talking, so I could never really tell if something was bothering him or if we was just taking in the scenery. Then I started thinking about the whole Daphne thing and then, maybe 'cause I was tired and hung over, all of a sudden I felt like if someone was to look me in the face just then they'd be able to tell I was hiding something and they'd ask me what was up my nose and I'd have to tell 'em. So I tried some more small talk with Johnny, but nothing but foolery come outta my mouth.

"That Daphne's a real peach, ain't she?" I says, lying like a rug. But it wouldn't do Johnny no good to tell him what she done.

"She's all right, I guess," he says.

"All right?" I says. "You ever seen a prettier sight?"

"I don't mean that way," he says.

"Then what?" I says.

"Well," he says, "it's just that she's an awful flirt. She's supposed to be Abel's girl."

You coulda knocked me over with a feather when he said that.

"You mean you saw her giving me the eye?" I says.

"She give you the eye, too?" he says real casual, without even turning my way.

"Now hold on just a minute, Johnny," I says. "You mean she winked at *you*?"

"'Course that's what I mean," he says. "And I suppose she kissed *you* also."

"She *kissed* you?" I says a little too loud. "When did this happen?"

"This morning, while everyone else was still asleep. I went into the kitchen to get something to eat. When I got there, Daphne comes in from outside and asks me to step outside for a minute, and so I went outside with her. Soon as the door closed behind us, she puts her arms around me and plants a big, sloppy kiss on me, on the mouth, no less."

I couldn't hardly believe my ears. It took me a minute to pull myself together. When I finally did, I asked him what happened after that.

"I pulled her off me and wiped her spit off of my face. She laughed and tried to kiss me again, but I pushed her away and told her to never try that again. Then I walked up here and watched the sunrise. Then you come out."

"I see," I says, feeling much better about the whole thing for some reason. "So whad'll you say to Abel about it?"

"Why, I won't say nothin'. I ain't *that* stupid. Abel's nuts about her, but he'll figure her out soon enough, so why get mixed up in it?"

I realized as he was telling me all this that I'd underestimated Johnny to the point where I felt like apologizing to him, but I couldn't 'cause there was no way to do it without hurting his feelings. I just stared at him.

"What are you lookin' at?" he says. "I did the right thing, didn't I?"

"'Course you did, Johnny," I says. "I just

didn't realize you knew yer way around women so well."

"Oh," he says. "I met a few ladies in my time."

"Yer time?" I says. "Hell, you was sixteen when you joined the army, and I been around you ever since. Where'd you meet all these women?"

"Damn, Boyd," he says. "What'ya think I was doin' while the rest of you fellers were wasting all your time playing stupid card games?"

Well, he had me there. Yessir, there was more to Johnny than any of us knew.

"What did you do when she kissed you?" he asks, giving me this real serious look.

"Uh, well," I says. "We was never alone for her to try." That was a lie, of course, but the words just came out before I knew it.

"Well, watch out if she ever does get you alone," he says, turning away and looking up at the sky. Then we hear the front door to the house open and shut and people talking in the house, so we went in and had some breakfast.

5

Worse than our run-ins with Daphne, though, was the fact that Dobbs still hadn't showed up. Well, now we was worried on account of Dobbsy's shoulder and all. He mighta fallen off his horse and got knocked out, or run into some a Randy's boys or a Comanche raiding party. It was still possible that he went back to town and tied one on and then rented a room to sleep it off in, but that was a real longshot. We all preferred to do our serious drinking as a group, especially Dobbsy, who liked to have a familiar audience around when he got going. So Red said he'd get some men to fan out and search the ranch, though it was such a big place that you couldn't count on finding him even if he was around.

Abel took Bill and Johnny—who was the best scout of all of us—to go and try to pick up

Dobbsy's trail even though there was always so many horses coming and going around Elsinore that any trail he mighta left likely got mixed in with a hundred others. Meanwhile, me and Lem headed into town to check there. As the two of us rode off, I told Lem about what happened with Daphne the night before. Once he got though laughing and I convinced him that I was serious, the smile dropped right off his face.

"But she and Abel looked like they were getting along fine," he says.

"That's just my point," I says. "What is she up to?"

"Maybe she didn't have the nerve to tell Abel she ain't in love with him no more, you know, letting him down easy," says Lem.

"Didn't you hear what I just told you?" I says. "The lady was making passes at me right under Abel's nose. I'd say she's got nerves of steel! No, she's up to something, all right."

We talked it over some more as we rode, keeping a lookout for signs of Dobbs as we went. When we got into Gonzago, we went into Wilson's to ask if anybody seen him.

Sitting at the bar was that Wendel feller, so we asked him if he seen Dobbsy around town at all. He told us no, but he would check around and see if anyone else spotted a stranger in town last night. He come running back in about ten minutes later, all outta breath.

"You find him?" says Lem.

"What?" he says. "Oh, your friend. No, no

one's seen him. But there's something more important goin' on that Abel's got to know about right away."

"Listen, Wendy, or whatever your name is," says Lem, standing up like he was gonna draw. "There ain't nothing more important than finding our friend."

Wendel took a couple steps backward and nearly tripped over a chair doing it.

"Easy, Lem," I says, putting my hand on his shoulder and sitting him down again. "Go ahead, Wendel, what was it you was gonna tell us?"

"Well," he says, leaning over the table and talking in a near whisper. "Turns out there *is* a stranger in town. He's got a room upstairs at Ferguson's. You know, the other saloon down the street. And who d'ya think it is?"

He paused, and we stared at him, waiting for him to finish.

"For chrissakes, Wendel," I says, "you gonna make us guess?"

"Ever heard of a feller named Doc Rivers?" he says, leaning back with a smile, like he just discovered America or something.

"'Course we have," I says. "Who hasn't hearda him? I'm a little surprised he bothered to stop in this backwater village you call home, but what's his being here got to do with Abel?"

"Whad'ya *think* he's doin' here?" says Wendel, throwing up his hands. "The word is Randy hired him to kill Abel."

Me and Lem looked at each other for a second, then we turned back to Wendel, who was all excited.

"You sure about this?" says Lem.

"Well, like I said," says Wendel, "that's the word around town, but you can count on it being true. So whad'ya gonna do?"

"Damn," Lem says to me. "Where the hell did Randy get the money to hire him? I'll bet he costs a small fortune, specially to come all the way out here."

"Musta been saving up," I says. "Wonder if Rivers still uses that big ol' Walker?"

"Nah," says Lem. "I'm sure he's using something a little lighter by now. You know, he ain't getting any younger."

"I don't believe this!" says Wendel, looking at us like we was insane. "Why ain't you two burnin' the breeze out to Elsinore to warn Abel 'stead of settin' around talking about hardware?"

"Easy, there, Wendel," says Lem. "First off, if Doc Rivers is here to kill Abel, he ain't gonna pull anything sneaky. He cares more about his reputation than he does about his own hide. He'll challenge Abel up front to a showdown. So relax."

"Relax?" says Wendel, jumping up. "Are we talking about the same Doc Rivers here? So what if he's up front about it. He's still gonna pass a bullet through Abel. And I hear he always goes for the heart."

"Aw, sit your ass down, Wendel," I says. "You're attracting attention. If Rivers is really here to shoot it out with Abel, then he's as good as dead right now—Rivers, I mean. See, Abel's not a man to make a big fuss about such things, but he just so happens to be as fast on the draw as any mother's son I ever seen. And he's about twenty years younger'n that Rivers feller, too. Anyway, it'll be an interesting match-up, won't it, Lem?"

"Can't wait," he says with a wink.

But the truth is, me and Lem was plenty worried about Abel having to go up against this Rivers feller. Not that Abel wasn't just as fast as we said he was, but sometimes these gunfights are tricky affairs—all kindsa things can go wrong. A man's gun can jam, or maybe he'll miss a vital spot and give the other feller the split second he needs—whatever. But if Doc Rivers came all the way out to Gonzago to duel it out with Abel, then that's likely the way it was gonna be, 'cause Abel sure warn't gonna turn tail and run, 'specially knowing Randy'd prob'ly ordered the headstone already.

Now, lemme just say a word or two about this Doc Rivers and gunfighters in general. I'm sure you read all kindsa stories and legends about these fellers that make 'em sound like heroes and such, and maybe a couple of 'em were fairly interesting characters at that. But most of 'em, including our friend Doc, really started out as nothing more'n hair-trigger troublemakers, the kinda feller you wouldn't so much as play a friendly game of poker with on account of their nasty tempers. What'd happen is that eventually they killed so many men over stupid things that they'd get a sorta reputation.

Well, word travels about a man being fast on the draw, so that by the time he walks into some saloon to wet his whistle, there's another trouble-making type of feller already there, sitting in the corner, just itchin' to make his reputation by being a little faster. And he'll pick a fight, of course, and the next thing you know he's laying on the ground with his gun halfway outta his holster, dead as a doornail, and the only thing he gets for his trouble is a reputation for being a complete idiot, until he's forgotten about a week later. The established man, though, *his* reputation just got a little bigger.

But the local marshall or sheriff will show up and tell the gunfighter he ain't welcome in town no more and to clear out, and so he goes someplace else and the whole fool process starts all over again. So, you see, all that being a famous gunfighter really means is you just end up drifting from place to place, with no friends on account of nobody wants to be caught in the crossfire when the next fight breaks out, until eventually someone does come along who's just a little faster and puts you six foot under the ground and there's no one to cry over you at your funeral. So there's your gunfighter. A friendless drifter living on borrowed time.

Anyway, this Doc Rivers was one of these fellers, and he figured he might as well make a little money on his way to the graveyard, so he started hiring out to people who wanted some-one else killed but who either warn't fast enough or didn't have the *cojones* to do the job themselves. In Randy's case, I reckon it was both.

"Well," says Wendel, getting up to go, "if you ain't worried, then I guess I ain't either. Just make sure Abel knows it was me that tipped you off. And if I hear anything about your missing friend, I'll let you know."

"Well?" says Lem after Wendel left. "What'll we do?"

"What can we do?" I says. "You know Abel ain't got no choice but to have it out with Rivers. If it was a coupla weeks ago, I wouldn't be so concerned. I'd have said he had a better'n even chance of winning. But with Dobbsy missing and Daphne on his mind . . ."

"I know," says Lem. "I was thinking the same thing. Well, there ain't nothing for it. Still, maybe we oughta just say a quick hello to Rivers and let him know who he's dealing with. Might give him something to think about."

"Couldn't hurt," I says.

I ain't sure what me and Lem thought we was gonna accomplish by going to see Rivers, 'cause everyone knowed that once a man like that took on a job, he finished it—if he didn't, his reputation would vanish into thin air, and, like I said, that's all his type cared about.

So we went down the street to Ferguson's.

We left our guns with the bartender, went upstairs, and knocked on his door.

"Who the hell's that?" says this cranky voice from inside. "I got the door covered, so you better open it real slow and lemme see your hands."

"Friends of Abel Braddock," I says, "and we just wanna talk, so hold your fire. We ain't armed."

I opened the door like he said to and walked into the room with my arms above my head, and Lem did the same behind me.

"Now kick the door shut and sit down over there on that sofa," says Rivers when we was inside. He was sitting up in his bed with a plate of food in front of him. He had long, almost-white hair, a hawk's beak for a nose, squinty gray eyes, and one of the bushiest moustaches I ever seen, which was also nearly white. He was a real skinny sonofabitch, even his face, and the fact that he was wearing all black made him look even thinner. He really looked like a harmless old codger, sitting there in bed like that, 'cept for the fact that he was aiming a coupla pistols in our direction with the steadiest hands you ever saw.

"I was right, Boyd," says Lem. "He ain't carrying around that heavy old Walker no more. They're Remington Armys."

"Yeah," I says. "Only now he's got one for each hand."

"All right, cut the gab," says Rivers. "My supper's gettin' cold. So you're friends of Abel

Braddock's, eh? That s'posed to mean something to me?"

"Rumor has it you're in town to do a job fer Randy Eckhardt," I says. "That right?"

"It's none of your damn business what I'm doin' here," he says.

"Easy, there, Doc," says Lem. "We just thought you oughta know what you're getting yourself into. See, Randy's considered a loser, even in this one-horse town, and it just don't seem right, a man of your stature, hiring out to a low-life the likes of him."

Rivers just sat there squinting at us for a few seconds, then suddenly burst out laughing, so hard, in fact, that the china on his tray started rattling.

"You think I give a goddamn who I hire out to?" he says. "Jesus, Mary, and Joseph, the people I work for pay me to kill, you idiots. You know any upstanding citizens who'd do a thing like that?"

"Maybe not," I says, "but in this particular case, you should know who it is you're being paid to shoot."

"Save it," says Doc, puttin' down one of his guns and taking a bite of meat and washing it down with a gulp of beer. "Abel Braddock, war hero, fought Indians for the United States Army after the war, came back home to run the family ranch. Did I leave anything out?" He took another bite of meat and sat there, chewing away with a big grin on his face.

"Only this," says Lem, who was getting as tired of the wrinkled ol' notcher as I was. "Abel Braddock come home from the army with some good friends who ain't gonna stand by and let some washed-up trigger man shoot him down and walk off with a filthy little pile of blood money."

Rivers stopped smiling, put down the joint of meat he was eating, and picked up his second pistol again.

"Listen, junior," he says, cocking his guns, "we both know I ain't washed up—you wouldn't bother coming here if I was, now, would you? Still, it don't sit well with me, having a punk like you say shit like that. I ought to plug you just on principle."

"I ain't afraid of you, old man," says Lem.

"No? You oughta be. And what about you, boy?" says Rivers, lookin' at me with a sly grin. "You afraid of me?"

"You know, pops," I says, "I think it's been too long since you faced any real competition if you think we scare that easy." Hearin' Lem stand up to the man kinda brought out the tough guy in me.

"Really, now," says Rivers. "And what makes you two so special?"

"Well," I says, "I guess you was too busy doing the dirty work of rats like Randy to know there was a war on a few years back, but when you get shot at for long enough, you kinda get used to the idea of dying. See, I know yer fast and all, but I just don't give a shit."

Rivers kept staring at me for a minute. I gotta admit I was impressed the way his guns didn't move a hair. That ain't easy to do.

"You know what I think?" he says finally, uncocking his guns and laying them down on the bed. "I think you two would be plenty scared if you hadn'ta left your guns downstairs. Fact is, everyone knows I never shoot an unarmed man. But you're smarter than you look, I'll give you that."

"Think what you want, Doc," says Lem. "Only remember this. You go through with this job for Randy, and I promise it'll be your last. Whether Abel shoots you or me or Boyd or one of our other friends, it don't matter. See, outside the army we're nobodies with no reputations to look out for, so we ain't all that particular about playing fair. Which means even if you do get Abel—which I wouldn't count on if I was you—there'll still be more of us than even you can handle. You won't leave this town alive."

Doc didn't so much as blink.

"If that's the way it pans out, so be it," he says, picking up a piece of bread and dipping it in some gravy. "I ain't washed up, but I am getting pretty old for a man in my line of work. I reckon Gonzago's as good a place to die in as any other. You tell your boss I'll do it any place he wants to, but I'd prefer right here in town. Better for my reputation if there's lots of witnesses. And close the door on your way out, would ya, boys?"

So we left him and went downstairs to pick up our guns.

"You know what I say, Boyd?" says Lem, looking up the stairs as he strapped on his holster and pulled out his gun. "I say let's you and me shoot the bastard right now. Hell, no one's gonna care how it happened."

"No one 'cept for Abel," I says. "C'mon, Lem, use your head—Abel'd have a fit and you know it. Nope, the only thing we can do now is let him know about it and hope he's faster, which I think he is."

"And if he ain't?" says Lem.

"Then he ain't. But meanwhile, you, me, Bill, and Johnny will be waiting off to the side to finish off Rivers if he does win—from behind, if need be."

Lem glanced upstairs one more time and put his pistol away.

"All right," he says, "but you better not change your mind about doing that sonofabitch in cold blood when the time comes."

"*If* the time comes," I says. "Don't forget, Abel ain't no slouch with a gun. Remember that time he took out four Yankees with three bullets?"

I had him now. Lem had to laugh at that one.

"You know, you're right. Goddamndest bit of shooting I ever saw," he says, slapping me on the back.

"And look on the bright side," I says. "Once we get through this, we won't have to worry about Randy ever again. Where's he gonna go from hiring Doc Rivers?"

'Course, I didn't really believe that Randy would ever stop, but sometimes a feller's gotta pretend things are better'n they really are, even to himself.

"C'mon," I says, "let's head back to the house."

By the way, the event I was referring to happened during the last weeks of the war. We was trying to withdraw from a skirmish with an enemy force that outnumbered us by about five to one when we got pinned down by some Union snipers, four of 'em, who were positioned above us on a cliff behind some trees. We was trying to crawl forward on our bellies when one of our officers got hit and was crying out in pain, and the snipers kept firing away at him, dirt flying up all round him. So Abel, who was senior to the wounded man and by rights should have stayed put, he takes a rifle and crawls forward near to where the other man was down until he gets a good angle to fire up at the snipers.

Well, they see him and start firing away like crazy at him, so he's only got a matter of seconds before they find their mark. So he shoots one, reloads, shoots another one, then realizes he's only got one other bullet with him. Meanwhile, the remaining two snipers start moving away from where they was to get some better cover, and just at the right moment, as they're real close to the edge of the cliff, Abel draws a bead on one and fires. He falls into the other one, who's nearest to the rim, and they both go falling off the edge and down into the ravine below. You never heard such cheering in your life. Every man in our unit watched the whole thing, and that's all we talked about right up till the surrender. Abel, of course, said it was just a lucky shot, but we knew better.

Me and Lem got back to Elsinore again and found out there was still no sign of Dobbsy. Johnny just couldn't pick up a trail. It was beginning to look bad. Then, soon as Daphne warn't around, we pulled Abel aside and told him about Doc Rivers.

"You're kidding!" he says, kinda excited. "The legendary Doc Rivers, all the way out here? Looks like Randy's run out of patience." Then he gets angry.

"All right, then," he says, getting to his feet. "That suits me fine, because I'm all out of patience myself. The little shit—you know, I'm half convinced Randy's got something to do with Dobbs disappearing, too."

"I agree," says Red, walking into the room all of a sudden. "I've been thinking that all day. Your friends don't strike me as the type of men who'd just go wandering off, and knowing Randy the way I do, well, I wouldn't put anything past him at this point. And did I hear someone mention the name of Doc Rivers?"

"Yeah, Randy's gone and hired him to gun down Abel," says Lem.

Red snaps his fingers when he hears this.

"So that's where it went."

"Where what went?" says Abel.

"Oh, only about fifteen hundred bucks which I noticed missing from the vault a couple days ago," says Red, getting all worked up. "It was really starting to bother me, because it didn't seem possible one of the hands took it—they know I'd line 'em right up against a wall if they ever stole so much as a penny from that safe. Now it all makes sense. I'll bet fifteen hundred is Doc Rivers' going rate these days. That little bastard, after all I've done to protect him! You know, he'd have been locked up a long time ago if it weren't for me. Gambling debts, liquor tabs. I even paid off the family of some poor local girl he forced himself on one drunken night. Cost me a fortune, that one. And now he steals from me—and to pay to have some lowlife kill the only real friend I got in the world? Well, that's it—it's over!"

Abel walks over to Red and pats him on the back.

"Easy, Red," he says. "You did your best, but you can't tame a rattlesnake. I don't think even Daphne will stand in the way at this point, not when she finds out what he's done."

"Too bad if she doesn't like it," says Red, still seething with anger. "She's a sweet girl and all, but you're my, you're family. Christ, Abe, if anything'd happened to you I could never have forgiven myself. You let me take care of this Doc Rivers business. Maybe if I tell him that money wasn't Randy's to spend—"

"Aw, come off it, Red," says Abel. "He couldn't care less whose money it is. No, I'll handle Rivers."

"Handle him?" says Red. "Handle him how? He's a goddamn killing machine, Abel. I won't let you do it."

"Red, I have no choice," says Abel, "and you know it."

"Yes, you do," says Red, with tears starting to well up in his eyes. "You can get the hell out of town, right now. You and your men. I'll give you all the horses and supplies you need. The Mexican border's not that far off, and besides, Rivers won't follow you once he hears you've left."

Abel just looked at Red and shook his head.

"Goddamn it, Abe," says Red, almost shouting. "Don't you think you've been playing the hero long enough? What, you think because you managed to come through the war alive that you're immortal or something? You're young—hell, you're still a kid, for chrissakes. You came back to Elsinore to finally start living your life again, and now you want to just throw it all away and let Randy win? That's what it'll mean, that Randy wins."

"I told you, Red," says Abel, "it's not what I want, it's what I've got to do." After that, Abel walks out of the house, leaving Red standing there staring out the door with his hands out in front of him, like he was begging or something.

"Can't you boys talk some sense into him?" says Red without turning around.

"Once Abel's made up his mind," says Bill, "that's it. Besides, Mr. Braddock, you never seen Abel shoot. He's a natural."

"Yeah," I says, feeling kinda sorry for Red. "That old has-been Rivers just met his match. Lem, tell Red about the time . . ."

"Aw, knock it off, will ya?" says Red. "We're talking about a man with twenty years of experience winning gun fights. Experience counts for everything in this world."

Then Red walks out of the room shaking his head. So me and Lem tell Bill and Johnny how we planned to ambush Rivers if Abel loses, and they agreed it was a good idea—a dirty, rotten, stinking, underhanded thing to do, but a good idea. 'Course, they wasn't any happier about the possibility of Abel getting killed than me and Lem was. Then Abel comes back inside and says if we're coming along to watch the big show-down, we'd better saddle up 'cause he was leaving in five minutes regardless. It was clear enough he wanted to get the whole thing over with as soon as possible, and that suited the rest of us just fine. So off we went.

6

As soon as we got back into town and people recognized us, a crowd started gathering on both
sides of the street. That was just what we
wanted, 'cause it'd be easier for me, Johnny,
Lem, and Bill to sorta blend in when the fight
started.

"Now listen up, the four of you," says Abel
with the sorta grim smile he got when he was giving us important orders. "I don't want any nonsense from you boys when the time comes."

"Whad'ya mean by that?" I says.

"I mean I don't want any help of any kind,"
he says. "Understood?"

"C'mon, Abel," says Lem. "We wouldn't
pull anything as low-down as that."

"I know you wouldn't," he says. "Not deliberately, anyway. Just keep your hands in your
pockets until it's over, okay?"

"Don't give it another thought, Abel," says Bill. "Just concentrate on putting one right between that feller's eyes so we can all go home."

"I'll do my best," says Abel, cool and calm like always. "Now, where can I find this—never mind, there he is."

We turn around and there he was, walking slow and steady toward us. He looked a lot taller standing up than he did up in his room, prob'ly 'cause he had his hat and boots on now. But he looked skinnier'n ever. Like before, he was dressed all in black, which, if you forgot for a second who it was, actually kinda made him look ridiculous. But then you saw those squinty eyes again, and suddenly he didn't look silly no more.

Abel steps out into the street and starts walking toward him, and the rest of us casually moved off into our positions, as far away from each other as we could get so as not to give Rivers easy targets. Lem was gonna wait in a little alley that ran between the saloon where Rivers was staying and the building next to it.

The two men got to within about thirty yards of each other and then stopped. Everyone that was still standing in the street now stepped off it, so that the sides were lined with people and the middle part was empty except for Abel and Rivers. I looked around at all the faces for a second, and suddenly I caught sight of Randy, kinda peekin' out from behind a big ol' post. Well, well, I thought, so much for him being sent up to Abilene.

Rivers pulled his coattails back behind his guns. It was all part of his little show, 'cause any normal feller woulda just left his damn coat off in the first place. Then both men kinda held their arms out at their sides so that their hands were only a few inches from the handles of their guns. Now I started gettin' nervous, like it was just hitting me what was about to happen. I went to lick my lips but I couldn't on account of how my mouth was so dry I couldn't get it open. It had got so quiet that all of a sudden I realized I could hear the wind. Then I saw River's right hand move just a hair—more like a twitch—and a split second later he was falling backward with a tiny black hole in his forehead and this real surprised look on his face.

Rivers slid to the ground, knees first, and I remember it seemed like I didn't hear the shot until then, but I musta heard it earlier 'cause they warn't far enough away for the sound to be delayed. Meanwhile, Rivers was still kneeling there on the ground, still looking surprised, only now blood was running from his forehead down the sides of his nose and into that big moustache of his. Then he just fell forward, face first into the dirt with a crunch, which was the sound of that nose of his breaking as it hit. But he didn't feel it 'cause he was already dead. Then the street was deathly silent again, and it stayed that way for a few seconds, till someone let out a hearty "Yee-ha!" which turned out to be Lem. Then all hell broke loose, and everyone rushed into the street to congratulate Abel, who hadn't moved from his spot.

Finally, the spit come back into my mouth, and I let out a long sigh. Then I look over to where Randy was before, but he was gone. So I walked over to Bill and Johnny, who were leaning against a rail in front of the dry-goods store, waiting for the crowd to break up that was all around Abel.

"Christ," says Bill with a big smile. "He really did put one between his eyes! That's one for the books, all right. I mean, Rivers didn't even get a hand on his gun!"

"Did either of you see Abel's hand move?" I says. "I swear, I didn't see it move he drew so fast."

"Yeah, that's how it looked to me, too," says Bill. "You see the look on Rivers' face? Oh, boy, was that good. I don't think he saw the hand move neither."

"I saw his hand move," says Johnny, looking back and forth at us. "You didn't see it move?"

"Wish I had your eyes, Johnny," I says, "'cause I only caught a blur. And how 'bout that Abel, putting the gun back in the holster right away. If I didn't know him better, I'd say he was showing off!"

Then Lem comes running over and says he couldn't see no movement neither. Then he holds up Rivers' brace of Remingtons.

"Souvenirs," he says. "You know Abel wouldn't want 'em. I was gonna take his hat, too, but someone else got it first. Hey, Abel!"

Abel comes over to where we was standing after getting his hand shook by about fifty people. He warn't happy, and he warn't sad, just calm.

"All right, boys," he says, "now we can get back to finding out what happened to Dobbs. Oh, and I saw what you boys were up to."

"Huh?" says Lem, overdoing the innocent routine. "What are you talking about?"

"I'm not angry," he says, "but you men ought to care more about your own good names, not to mention the law. The marshall here tolerates a fair fight, but he would've been all over you boys if you'd gone through with that little ambush of yours."

Damn, I thought, you couldn't get nothin' past Abel. Man's about to shoot it out with Doc Rivers and still he's got the wherewithal to notice we was up to something.

"Now, Abel," says Lem, putting his arm around Abel's shoulder, "what's important is that you won—and we knew you would. But let's say your gun jams or something. Knowing how fast that Rivers feller was, he woulda shot you anyway, so we woulda been within our rights to open up on him."

"How so?" says Abel, looking as puzzled as the rest of us.

"Well," says Lem, "after all, a man with a gun that don't work is just another way of saying an unarmed man, and Rivers himself told us that shooting unarmed men was taboo."

Abel finally broke a smile and shook his head.

"Lem," he says, "in the seven years we've been together, has a gun ever jammed on me?" It was true. Abel was lucky that way, too.

"Coulda happened is all I'm sayin'," says Lem.

So after listening to Lem hem and haw for a couple more minutes, we went and had a drink with what seemed like the whole town of Gonzago, and then headed back to Elsinore.

On the way, Abel asks if any of us saw what become of Randy after the fight, but nobody seen where he went.

"I knew he'd never actually go up to Kansas with me around. Maybe Red'll have an idea where to find him," says Abel. "I've still got a hunch that Randy or some of his hirelings either ran into Dobbs and killed him or deliberately snatched him and are holding him somewhere."

"Your hunches are never wrong," I says. "Only I sure hope they're holding him," I says. "But either way, Randy's a dead man." When I said that, Abel just shrugs.

"You are gonna go and plug him," I says, "ain't you Abel? I mean, after we find Dobbsy, of course, but you are gonna pay him back, right?"

"That'll take care of itself in good time," says Abel.

I didn't like the sounda that, and neither did the rest of us. Abel was gonna bend over backwards to avoid killing Randy just to please that witch Daphne. I was real close to telling him about her flirting with me and Johnny, but I just couldn't do it.

"On the other hand," says Bill, "the way Red was carrying on before about Randy, it'll be a miracle if *he* ain't killed him by the time we get back."

"Jesus," says Abel. "I forgot about that."

"Maybe Red don't know Randy never went to Abilene," says Lem.

"Maybe," says Abel. "C'mon, we better hurry!"

So we rushed back at full gallop, and when we got there Red was sitting on the front steps of the house with a bottle. When he sees Abel, he looks up at the sky and closes his eyes.

"You did it!" he shouts, getting to his feet and then falling back down on account of being drunk. "You know, I actually prayed for the firsht time in my life thish afternoon? Reckon I'll have to start goin' to church reg'lar now."

"Red," says Abel as he tied up his horse, "I appreciate you praying for me and all, but please tell me you haven't done anything with Randy while I was gone."

"Randy?" says Red looking kinda crosseyed. "Naw, he's all yoursh, pal. But you'll give him one for me, won't ya? Give him one for good ol' Uncle Red." He starts to take another drink, and Abel snatches the bottle away. Red looks down at his empty hand and starts laughing.

"All right, Uncle Red," says Abel, pulling

Red to his feet and taking an arm around his shoulder. "Let's get you inside. Gimme a hand, will you Johnny?"

They lay Red down in one of the bedrooms and close the door. Just then, Daphne walks in from outside.

"Abel!" she says, running into his arms, all teary-eyed. "You're not going to face that horrible man, do you hear?"

"Uh, Ma'am," says Bill, "if you mean Doc Rivers, he already did."

"What?" says Daphne, pulling herself away from Abel. "And you're all right? Oh, thank God! To hear Red go on and on, anyone would have thought—but you're all right. Thank God for that." Then she starts hugging him again.

"Listen, Daphne," says Abel, grabbing her by the shoulders. "I need to know where Randy is. I just want to talk to him, I swear."

"Randy?" she says, wiping her eyes with a handkerchief. "Red sent him up to Kansas with a herd. I saw them leave the other day."

"Yes, I know," says Abel, "the herd went, and the rest of the men, but Randy stayed behind. We saw him in town just a little while ago. I don't know if Red told you, but—"

"He told me," she says, turning away like it hurt to even think about it. "I know Randy was the one who hired that Doctor Rivers person. And I also know he tried to get some other men to kill you, too. Oh, Abel, I love him, I do, but he's, he's not right in the head. He's always been difficult, even when he was a little boy, you remember. But ever since Papa died, he's become such a bad person—worse than you know. And when I heard you were coming home, even though I couldn't wait to see you, I knew Randy wouldn't be able to control himself. But I'm such a little fool, I thought maybe things would work out—how, I don't know. I guess I didn't really think it through at all."

"It's not your fault, Daff," says Abel. "And it's not Red's, either. You both did what you could. I suppose it's not even Randy's fault, really."

"Oh, Abel," she says, laughing and crying at the same time. "You're still the sweet, kind boy you were before you left, for you to still have any compassion for him after what he's done. But I agree with Red. It's got to stop, once and for all. I can't protect him from himself any longer. No one can."

All this time, me and Bill and Lem were sitting there, kinda uncomfortable at having to listen to someone else's family problems and feeling like we was intrudin', but when I went to get up and leave at one point, Abel made that tiny motion with his hand that meant stay right where you are. On the other hand, we woulda had to drag Johnny from the room. He was leaning forward, eager to hear every word.

"We'll see, Daphne," says Abel. "But right now, I need to find him because we think he might know where our missing friend is. Do you have any idea where Randy might hide out—what about at your father's place?"

"The house?" she says. "No, I just came from there myself. His horse wasn't in the stable, either."

"And you can't think of anywhere else he might be?" says Abel. "Any other buildings on the property here?"

"No," she says, "there really isn't anyplace he could go without being seen. Except for the old barn out back here, every building on the whole ranch is being used for one thing or another."

"Well, we checked the barn," says Abel, who was getting mad again. "I should've had one of you follow him when he left town."

"Sorry, Abel," says Lem. "Maybe if we'd been using our heads instead of worrying about getting Rivers—"

"Forget it," says Abel. "It's water under the bridge now. Daff, does Randy have any friends in Gonzago?"

"A couple, maybe," she says. "But since your father died, most people around here have gotten kind of chilly toward Randy and me because we still associated with Red after the rumors started up about him. You know the ones—"

"Yeah, I know," says Abel. "Can you remember any names, anybody Randy might have mentioned?"

"Let's see," she says. "There was Jimbo McCullock, but they had a big fight a few weeks ago. But I'll bet he'd know of anyone else."

"Great," says Abel. "Come on, boys."

Except for Daphne, we all went out to the stable. When we got inside, Abel pulls us all together into a circle.

"All right, now," he whispers. "I'm going to stay here with Johnny and, and keep an eye on things. I want you three to go back into town and look up Jimbo and see if he can help. But on the way, I want you to take a little detour and check out the old Eckhardt place anyway. That road that intersects this one, about two miles down, take a left and it'll take you right to the house."

"But wouldn't Daphne have seen anything if she just came from over there?" says Bill. Bill still didn't know what me and Johnny and Lem knew about Daphne. But I was mighty relieved to hear that Abel was starting to have his suspicions.

"That's right, she would have. But check it out anyway. And be careful. There shouldn't be anyone there but a Mexican house maid. If it looks even a little suspicious, you come straight back here and get us. Don't go trying to save the day by yourselves."

So the three of us started for town and turned left at the crossroad like Abel said to. I told Bill what me and Lem already knew about Daphne, and after about a half hour's ride we could see the house up ahead. I coulda sworn I saw a figure crouching on the roof and then run behind a chimney.

"You see that?" I says, slowing down to a trot.

"There's someone on the roof," says Lem.

"I didn't see anything," says Bill.

"Well, we did," says Lem. "So what'll we do? If we turn around now, whoever it is will know we spotted 'em."

"Let's ride up and knock at the door," says Lem. "If the maid answers, we'll say we was looking for Daphne. Meantime, keep a sharp lookout for anything weird."

We tried knocking, but nobody answered. So I opened the front door and yelled, "Anybody home? Daphne?" No answer. But just then we all heard a floorboard creak somewhere inside. That settled it. Someone was there, all right.

"Guess she ain't around," I says, loud enough for whoever it was to hear. "C'mon fellers, let's head on into town. Maybe she's there."

"That ties it," I says when we got far enough away to talk. "Either Randy's hiding out in there or they got Dobbs. Hopefully, both. And whatever's going on, that Daphne knows all about it. We better go back and tell Abel right away."

When we passed this spot on the trail where it forked off toward some hills, Lem stopped short and told us to hold up. He dismounted and walked a few paces down the other trail, leaned over, and picked up something blue and white. It was a woman's shawl.

"What's this doing out in the middle of nowhere, I wonder?" says Lem. "It's silk. Not the kind of thing a woman would drop without going back to pick it up. Unless, of course, they was being chased. And look, it's got some blood on it."

"Where do you suppose this trail leads to? Uh-oh," says Bill, getting down close to the ground to look at something. "These hoof prints along here," he says. "I don't like to say it, but they look like—"

"Comanche ponies," says Lem.

"But didn't Red say the local Comanches are a peaceful bunch?" I says.

"He did," says Lem. "But forget that for a minute. What I'm thinking is a party of white folks getting shot at and riding for their lives might leave a pretty silk scarf laying on the ground, but the Indians chasing them sure as hell woulda come back for it. It's just the kind of thing they go nuts over. There's something strange going on around here."

"If they're just out for blood," I says, "maybe they warn't paying attention to the goodies the folks they attacked was carrying."

"Yeah, right," says Lem. "You know Indians ain't like that. The most bloodthirsty redskin that ever lived wouldn't pass up a trophy like this."

"Aw, forget your dumb theories, you two," says Bill. "Ain't none of us an expert on Indian ways, especially the Comanches. Besides, there's some folks who might be in trouble. Let's follow these tracks and see for ourselves."

So we followed the trail. After nearly an hour, we saw a thin plume of smoke about a mile

up the trail, which we figured probably was coming from a Comanche village, so we tied up our
horses and kept going on foot.

Finally, we come up over a small ridge and
saw what we was looking for, a big ol' Comanche
camp. But we couldn't tell if there was any white
folks down there or not without getting closer,
which we couldn't do without riskin' being spotted and all hell breaking loose. They mighta
been peaceful and all, but if they caught us
sneakin' around near their village they'd be sure
to get the wrong idea.

"Well, now what?" says Lem. "There's way
too many for the three of us to handle."

"Yeah, and even if we could," says Bill, "we
don't even know if this bunch has anything to do
with what we found back there. Hell, we don't
know if anything even happened to anyone.
What if they traded for that scarf and they just
dropped the damn thing by mistake? And don't
go tellin' me Indians never drop things. They
ain't all perfect, you know."

"What about the blood?" says Lem.

"Aw, for cryin' out loud," says Bill. "Maybe
the lady it belonged to cut herself slicing bread,
used the scarf to stop the bleeding, and then figured she could get some dumb Indian to buy it.
How should I know? Can't go starting up a war
with the Comanches over nothing, especially
without Abel giving the word. And Red might
have something to say about it, too. These could
be friends of his. I say we hightail it back to

Elsinore and let Abel and Red make the decision. Plus we oughta let Abel know about the Eckhardt house."

"All right, but that scarf's still bothering me," says Lem. "We know from the tracks they came this way. Maybe one of us should go back and the other two stay here and keep an eye on that village."

"Are you outta yer mind?" I says. "It'd be dark by the time we got back here, and with everything that's going on, splitting up would be the worst thing we could do. Besides, Abel'd have our hides for doing such a fool thing without more to go on than a bloody scarf."

"He's right," says Bill. "We can't do anything here till we talk to Abel and get a few more guns on our side anyway. Let's get the hell back."

So we walked back to where we hid our horses, but couldn't seem to find the spot. Finally, we realized they was gone. Well, now the three of us was in some pretty shit. Firstly 'cause whoever took our horses knew we was around, and secondly on account of us being a good fifteen miles from the ranch and even further from town. We had no choice but to go back on foot and hope we got there before dark.

"So, who woulda taken our horses? Any ideas, genius?" says Bill, looking over at Lem.

"Who would steal somebody's horse?" says Lem, scratching his head. "Hmmm, let me think. I dunno, Bill. Horse thieves?"

"I'm serious, you jackass!" says Bill.

"Well, it couldn'ta been those Comanches, now could it?" says Lem. "Not those peaceable, silk-scarf-tradin' Comanches back there. I mean, just because they're queer for horses don't mean they'd steal someone else's."

"All right, you two," I says. "It's gonna be a long enough walk without having to listen to that the whole way. It mighta been Comanches and it might not. But as I recall, they don't like the kinda horses we ride anyhow."

"No," says Lem, pissed I was taking Bill's side, "but they can sell 'em, though. And with the money they got they could buy themselves a whole wagonload of silk scarves!"

And so we kept on arguing like that for a minute, when all of a sudden a shot whistled over our heads. We all spun around with our guns drawn in the direction it came from, and there, sitting on horseback on a little grassy hill above us was about twenty Comanche warriors, all pointing their rifles at us. One of 'em yelled something and made a motion that we knowed meant "Drop your guns or we'll fill you full of lead." We obliged, of course, and soon they had us roped and were pulling us back toward the village.

7

When we got there, they sorta corralled us into the middle of their camp and made us kneel down in front of a big teepee. The women were staring at us and giggling among themselves, but the warriors were looking at us like we was lower than the lowest rat that ever scurried out from under a pile of garbage. These boys was the real thing, most of 'em over six foot, lean and mean, with faces that reminded me of birds of prey, you know, with that look of cold concentration in their eyes, like all they saw was their next victim.

Then the warrior closest to the big teepee pulls the flap open, and out comes what looked like the man in charge of the place. 'Course, the Indians don't really have the kind of leaders we do. They have chiefs and medicine men and such, but it ain't like in the white societies, where if someone in authority gives an order, the feller who disobeys gets punished. But they do have leaders, and you coulda told this feller was one even without all the fuss they was making over him. So this chief looks us over for a minute and then, in a booming voice, says in perfect English, "Why have you come here?"

Well, we was real surprised at that. The only Indians we ever run into up north that spoke any English were the Sioux and Cheyenne who lived off government handouts and never strayed more'n a mile or so from the agency. Hearing this man, a wild Comanche, speak our own language—and better'n I could, too—it was a real shock.

"Are you Many Horses?" says Bill.

"I have asked you a question," he says.

"We work on the ranch nearby," says Bill, who I guess decided he was gonna speak for the three of us. "We found the scarf that's in my back pocket on the trail near the road that runs to the ranch. You can see it has blood on it—when we saw the hoof prints of Comanche horses nearby, we thought one of our own might be in trouble, so we followed the trail here. We watched your village from that ridge up to the right, and when we saw that everything was quiet here, we left."

The old warrior had one of his men fetch the scarf from Bill's pocket. He looked it over, smelled it, and threw it down in front of Bill. He was smiling, but it warn't a happy smile, if you know what I mean.

"I will not talk of agreements your people

have had with other nations, and what has happened to them. I know about them, but I will not speak of them. My only concern is for my own people, who are at peace with your government," he says. "We signed a treaty that says we will make no war and kill no settlers and in return we will be allowed to use the land we have used for many generations, to hunt, to ride, to live as we have always lived. I wish to keep the agreement, but you white men will not let me.

I had once a very great friend who was of your people. It was he who taught me to speak your language. He was a white man, yet he was a wise and honorable man. He once saved my life, and twice I saved his. But when your people fought their great battle among themselves several years ago, my friend went to fight and never returned. I am sure he met a brave death, so his dying does not make me sad. What saddens me is that there does not seem to be any more honorable white men. I fear he was the only one, and if that is so then there can be no hope for my people. Only honorable men have the strength to honor their promises."

I have to tell you that listening to the man talk made me feel kinda strange. It was soothing, like listening to a river, or the rain on a tin roof. I turned toward Bill and Lem, and they both had a sorta dazed look on their faces. It warn't just his voice, though that was a big part of it. Each word seemed to hum after he spoke it. But it was what he was saying, too.

He stopped for a minute and looked off toward the west. The sun was getting low, and it turned his face a deep, brownish red. The reflection of the sun in his black eyes looked like two flames. Then he looked down at us again.

"My name is Many Horses. You feared that some of your people were in danger, and you followed the trail that leads to our village," he says. "I tell you that none of my people has harmed a white person or taken any of their property for several years now. It is true, there are Comanches many miles to the south and east of here who are not at peace with your people. But I cannot answer for them. And I do not know anything about that," he says, pointing to the scarf. "Yet if what you say is true, it was a brave thing for you to come here. You may speak."

"Many Horses, I swear to you that what I said is true," says Bill. "We only thought someone might be in trouble. We're not so brave. It's just that we're soldiers, or used to be. And we sure didn't have any intention of disturbing your village."

"I think I believe you," he says. "You are brave men, and you seem to be honest. Yet you tell me you work on the ranch nearby. You see, I am desperate to prove myself wrong about the white man."

"I'm not sure I understand, Many Horses," says Bill.

"There are other men from that ranch who have come here," says Many Horses, the anger rising up in his voice, "and those men wish to take what is ours. Several times they have come in great numbers with many long guns, pretending that they want more land for their cows to graze on, but I know what it is they truly seek. Even though they outnumbered us, my warriors could have easily defeated them. But I will not permit my people to dishonor themselves by breaking the treaty first. They have even stolen some of our horses, yet I will not allow my warriors to retaliate. How can you work on the ranch and yet know nothing of this?"

When Many Horses said that about men from the ranch coming here, the three of us kinda looked at each other for a second, wondering what the hell was going on.

"Many Horses, we only just arrived here a few days ago," says Bill. "We came with our friend, a very honorable and brave man called Abel Braddock, the son of the man who started the ranch. He has been away for many years, and now he has come back to take over the ranch. But I promise you, whatever has happened while he was gone he knows nothing about. And I also promise you that he is a just man who wants only peace between our people and yours."

Many Horses stood there for a second, eyein' Bill real carefully, like he was trying to see into his head if he was lying.

"This may be," he says finally.

"It is the truth, I swear to you," says Bill. "But tell me, Many Horses, what did you mean when you said you knew those other men weren't really after your land? If not land, then what?"

"They wanted the land, not for grazing, but for a thing that is on the land," says Many Horses.

"And what's that?" says Bill.

Many Horses paused again, looking kinda suspicious.

"A sacred place," he says. "A place that had been special to my people for a long time, since before my grandfather was born. I cannot tell you more than that. But I know that it is the reason the ranch men want the land my people use."

"Many Horses," says Bill, "if you let us leave in peace, we will return to the ranch and tell our friend Abel Braddock what you have told us. The ranch belongs to him, and because he is just and peaceful he will be very angry with the men who have come here with guns to steal your land. They will not be allowed to bother you anymore."

"It was always my intention to let you leave in peace," says Many Horses, "even if I did not believe you." Then he says something in Comanche to his warriors, and they untie us.

"There are your horses," says the chief, pointing to the other side of the village. "If you ride fast, you will make it to your ranch before it is dark, but you must go now."

"Thank you, Many Horses," says Bill. By the way, my name is Bill Evans, this here is Boyd McKenzie, and that's Lem Massey."

Many Horses nodded and shook each of our hands. I never shook the hand of an Indian before that, but you just had to like this Many Horses feller. The rest of the warriors still looked at us like we was dirt, even though they could see their chief was getting all friendly with us. But as long as the big man was on our side, it didn't matter.

"I hope all you say is true, Bill Evans," says Many Horses as we mounted up. "Then perhaps we can meet again as friends. But I must warn you. We will be peaceful only so long as we are allowed to live in peace."

"Agreed," says Bill. "One other thing, Many Horses. Will you allow our friend Abel Braddock to come and talk to you if he needs to?"

"Certainly," he says. "If he is the kind of man you say he is, I would welcome his friendship. Farewell."

"Farewell," says Bill, and off we rode.

8

"So," says Lem as we got to the main road, "that was quite a bit of smooth talkin' back there, Bill. Boyd, you ever hear him talk up such a storm before?"

"I think being around Abel and Dobbsy's worn off on him," I says. "When we first met him, you couldn't get a word outta him to save your life."

"Well, one of us had to say something," says Bill, "and I was damned if I was going to let either one of you open your traps and get us killed."

"Hardy-har-har," I says. "But seriously, boys, whad'ya suppose this sacred place is all about?"

"Beats me," says Bill. "Could just be some spring or something. You know how the Indians are about nature. Remember that tree shaped like a man that those Cheyenne warriors almost killed us over? Probably something like that."

"And what about this posse from the ranch trying to intimidate them?" says Lem. "Why would they risk stirring up bad blood with those Comanches over a spring? I mean, water's pretty scarce around here, but Snake Creek runs across the northern part of the ranch, right? And I don't know if you noticed, but those were some pretty fierce looking warriors back there."

"I'm sure it's Randy's doing, like Red told us," says Bill. It's probably got nothing to do with the sacred place or the land, just that goddamn pain in the ass Randy trying to make trouble. If Abel doesn't shoot the little prick soon, I'll do it myself. I swear I will."

"You'll have to beat me to the draw, partner," says Lem.

"Likewise," I says.

Well, we did just get back to Elsinore by sundown. As we approached the house, we could see through a window that Abel and Johnny and Red were sitting at the table with Daphne, so we decided we'd better just say we spent the day asking around about Randy and didn't find nothing, and then tell Abel everything soon as Daphne warn't around.

We put our horses away and went inside to eat, hungry as hell, and let Lem tell our little story. Daphne was all ears, and so was Abel, though we could tell he knowed we was full of it just from the way he nodded his head slightly with every detail—Abel never nodded when he was paying attention for real. Meanwhile, Red just kept rubbing the back of his neck on account of his hangover.

"Jesus, Lem," he says softly, "must you shout like that? We're right across the table from you, you know."

"And nobody in town had any idea at all where Randy might be?" says Daphne, getting up to clear the plates. "Not even Jimbo?"

"Nope," says Lem. "I'll tell you, I'm beginning to lose hope for Dobbsy."

"Oh, you mustn't do that," says Daphne. "Why just this morning Red and I thought our Abel was doomed to be shot down by that awful man." Then she walks up to Abel from behind and puts her arms around him. "And yet, here he is, alive and well, and I thank the Lord for that. I'll never give up hope again."

"She's right, boys," says Red, getting up with one hand on the table to steady himself and the other across his forehead. "We'll find him. Now if you'll all excuse me, I'm turning in. Night, everyone."

So we all hit the hay, but not before signaling to Abel when Daphne left the room that we needed to talk in private as soon as possible.

Next morning before sunup, Abel roused everyone 'cept Red and Daphne, and the five of us went to the stable and started saddling up as quiet as we could. Just as we're about to lead our horses outside, Slim comes walking in.

"Well, now," he says, looking kinda surprised. "Gettin' an early start, are we?"

"That's right, Slim," says Abel. "Time's running out for our missing friend. If he's outdoors somewhere, hurt and unable to travel, he'll be starving to death before too long, so every hour counts."

"Sure," says Slim. "You're absolutely right. Gonna keep searching the ranch area? If you are, don't bother north of here. We covered that part pretty good, and there ain't many trails that way anyhow. Your best bet is south and east. The terrain is hilly. Lots of little dips and gullies where an unconscious man could easily have been missed by our search parties. I'm gonna send out a bunch more west of here soon as it's light. Anyway, good luck."

"Thanks, Slim," says Abel. "Tell Red when he gets up we'll come back in the early afternoon for some grub and fresh horses." "Will do," says Slim, waving and walking toward the house.

"All right, talk," says Abel as soon as we were on our way.

After we told him everything, he thought about it for a minute or so. We could tell the news about the funny business at the Eckhardt house hit him hard 'cause it obviously meant Daphne was mixed up with whatever Randy was pulling. At least now we didn't have to say nothing about her making passes at us, I thought.

"Well, first we go straight to the Eckhardt house," he says. "What excuse do we use?" says Lem.

"None. We go in and search the place," says Abel.

This time, we didn't see nobody on the roof as we got near. Abel practically jumps off his horse out front, walks up and bangs on the front door. There was no answer, so he opens the door and walks in, and we all followed, 'cept for Johnny, who stayed outside to keep a lookout.

We searched all the rooms and found no sign of Dobbsy or Randy or anything out of the ordinary.

"I had a feeling we wouldn't find anything," says Abel. "They must've decided to play it safe after you boys showed up yesterday. Wait a minute."

Abel turned around, thinking about something, then starts running out of the house.

"Come on," he says. "There is another place we haven't checked."

We rode back the way we came, following Abel, who veered off the path to the left before we got back to the main road.

"Hey, Abel," says Johnny. "Do you see the fresh tracks?"

"Yep," says Abel. "Looks like we're onto something. There's an old ruin of a Spanish settlement up ahead. Me and a friend of mine used to ride out there sometimes when we were kids. Just a couple of small stone buildings, but a pretty good hideout. But it's set into a depression, so there's a blind spot or two. It's only another mile or so. We'll go off the trail a little ways before we get there and try to sneak up from the other direction."

We took it slow over some rough ground till we got to the bottom of a row of scrub-covered hills that rose up steeply above a little clump of trees, where Abel told us to tie up. We walked up the nearest hill, and when we got near to the top we got down on our hands and knees and crawled between the bushes to stay out of sight.

Finally, the ground starts sloping away from us, and soon we could make out the tops of the little stone buildings a few hundred yards below us. We took a route that'd bring us closest without being in sight of the buildings until we was nearly on top of 'em. We each hid behind our own bush and peeked down at the place, which was no more than a hundred feet away, and could see there was only one lookout, standing on top of a wall next to one of the buildings and facing away from us.

"Some lookout," whispers Lem. "Lookin' in the wrong direction. Where does Randy get these fellers, anyway?"

"All right, listen up," whispers Abel. "We can take these idiots by surprise. Johnny, you take care of the lookout with your knife, but wait for the rest of us to get right up to that far wall, and then on my signal." Johnny nodded.

We all bellied forward in the hot sand without making a sound. The wall the lookout was standing on, which formed a big unbroken square, was actually part of the little building we was gonna storm, and the door to the thing was on the other side of the wall, so we'd have to climb over it to get in.

When we was close enough to hear talking from inside the building, I spotted a huge rattlesnake slithering toward Johnny over to my left. Everyone sees it and stops moving. Shit, I thought, if that thing rears back and starts that infernal racket them things make, it'll mess up our whole operation. But Johnny sees it coming at him and just lies perfectly still, waiting. Good, I figured, he's gonna let the thing just go right by him. But then it starts veering toward Johnny's face, and just as its head is about a foot away from Johnny's nose, he grabs the snake's neck with one hand, crushing it flat and, as the body whips around, grabs the rattle with the other hand before the thing can give it a good shake and holds it till the body stops twitching. Bill and Lem couldn't see from where they was, but Abel looks over at me and smiles.

A minute later, we was all in position, and Abel gives Johnny the signal. Johnny lifts his body up with his left arm just high enough to give him throwing room, and with his right he flings his knife at the lookout. It lands square between the poor feller's shoulders. He tries to reach back and pull it out, but ends up falling backward off the wall and lands with a soft thud, burying the ten-inch knife right up to the hilt so the blade is sticking out his throat on the other side. Then, on another signal from Abel, the rest of us jump up and over the wall and run inside, guns out and yellin' to try and confuse whoever was in there.

Inside, propped up against a wall, was Dobbsy, trussed up like a pig, with a gag over his mouth. Across the room from him was two pathetic-lookin' guards, who both yell, "Don't shoot! Don't shoot!" and put their hands up as soon as we enter.

Dobbsy was alive, but just barely. His eyes were glassy and almost swollen shut from being smacked around, and he was pale as a ghost, probably from hunger. His shoulder bandages was gone, but the wound looked all right, though that was the least of his worries, the way he looked. As we took the gag off him, he smiles weakly at us and then closes his eyes.

Abel props his head up and gives him some water outta his canteen. Then he takes the hats offa the two guards and puts them under Dobbsy's head like a pillow. Then he turns around with an angry face and asks the guards who they work for, and they tell us Randy.

"When's your relief coming?" says Abel.

"Not till this afternoon," says one of 'em.

"And where's Randy?" says Abel. "Is he supposed to be here later?"

"We don't know," says the other one. "He might. They don't tell us nothin'. What're ya gonna do to us?"

"Shut up, you!" says Lem, spitting in the man's grimy, sweaty, fat little face. "We ain't figured that out yet. But you better hope that man don't die!"

"But we ain't the ones who beat him up," whines fat face, "Honest! Randy done that himself."

"Yeah," I says. "And I guess that means you two watched him do it."

Abel motions for us to lay off and then asks them what they do for food. One of them nods at a bag in the corner. Inside was a loaf of bread and some jerky.

"Boyd," says Abel, tearing off a chunk of bread and handing it to me, "try to feed Dobbsy some of this. Soak it in water first. Lem, cut up the jerky into small pieces and soak that, too."

We managed to get a little food into Dobbsy, but he kept passing out.

"All right, we gotta get him back to the house," says Abel. "Johnny, you and Bill strap Dobbsy to one of these fellers' horses and ride the other ones yourself. Just follow that trail out front. It leads right to the main road. The rest of us will go back the way we came. We'll try to meet you where the trail crosses the road, but if we're not there when you get there, just keep going straight back to the house and have Red call the doctor when you get there. And be ready for trouble while you're traveling, in case these two are lying."

So we saw Johnny and Bill off with poor old Dobbsy tied to a horse like he was a dead body or something, but there was no other way. Then we

led our two captives back with us to where we
left our horses.

"Don't you boys think for a minute that
we're gonna let you *ride* back," says Lem as he
pushes them ahead of him. "We got the horses,
all right, but you're walkin' it, understand? And
barefoot! Now move it!"

Well, Lem was just saying that to be mean,
but me and Abel let 'em think Lem was serious
'cause we was good and pissed. Even though we
was mighty pleased that we found Dobbsy alive,
we warn't sure if he'd even survive the ride
home.

Anyway, we got to the main road only a
short while after Johnny and Bill, so we caught
up with them and rode back together from
there without running into any trouble and
made it all the way back with Dobbsy still
breathing.

Back at the house, no one was around at first,
but then Slim come walking up. He says Red's
down the other end of the ranch and wouldn't be
back for a couple hours. So Abel had Slim go
fetch the doctor. Then we laid Dobbsy down on a
bed and waited for Slim to get back. I went outside with Abel, and we asked our prisoners again
where Randy was hiding out, but they either
didn't know or was playing dumb.

We had 'em sitting on the ground, tied back
to back, and I guess 'cause we hadn't killed 'em
or made good on any of our threats, they were
feeling confident enough to start complaining.

"Hey, you gonna give us any water?" says Fat Face. "It's a hundred degrees out here."

"Yeah," says the other one. "And how 'bout somethin' to eat? Any of that jerky left?"

"You know, Boyd," says Abel, "I don't think these two are taking their situation very seriously, do you?"

Well, I thought, this don't sound like Abel's usual style, but I'll play along.

"You know, Abel," I says, "you're right. Here they are worried about food and drink with their sorry asses on the line. I think they think we're bluffing."

"Let's show 'em we're not," says Abel. I had no idea what he meant, so I let him make the first move. And boy, did he ever. He walks over to where there was a stack of firewood at the side of the house, squats down, and looks at the ground real careful. Then he comes back over, tells me to give him a hand, and starts pulling our two friends over by their ropes toward the woodpile, so I pitched in. He says, "All right, that'll do," when we got about five feet away from the wood. Then he goes into the house and comes out with a jar of honey.

"Is that your idea of somethin' to eat?" says Fat Face. "I hate honey."

"Shut up, greaseball," I says, doing my best imitation of Lem. Then Abel starts pouring honey all over their two heads, down their fronts and onto their bare feet. Then he picks up a big stick and starts whacking the ground next to them. And then I knowed what he was up to.

"Hey Lem!" I shouted. "Better get out here. You gotta see this!"

By the time Lem come running out, it'd started. First a trickle, and then a flood of big, red, angry fire ants starts pouring outta a hole near the woodpile and heading right for our prisoners. They started pleading with us like scared children, but Abel just stood there with no expression on his face. Lem, on the other hand, looked like he died and went to heaven.

"Boyd," he says, slapping his knee, "you done right to call me out here, 'cause I woulda never forgiven you if you didn't!"

Meanwhile, the ants was already covering their feet, and they was in agony, screaming and hollering.

"Now then," says Abel, calm as ever. "Boyd, fetch me that can of turpentine in the kitchen. So I did, and handed it to him.

"You boys might think you're in pain now," says Abel, "but if I let those ants start crawling on your faces, into your ears, your mouths—they'll start into your eyeballs, eventually—if I let that happen, you'll be begging for us to shoot you."

"Make 'em stop!" screamed Fat Face, looking down in terror at the fire-ant shoes he was now wearing. "Oh, merciful God, make 'em stop." His friend was just plain screaming, no words at all, just, "Aaaaahhhhh! Aaaaahhhhh! Aaaaahhhhh!"

"Tell me where Randy is," says Abel. "Tell me now, and I'll pour this turpentine over your heads. It'll sting some, specially the eyes, but it's nothing compared to a head full of fire ants. Well? Better hurry, or you'll be like your friend there and I won't be able to understand you."

"The L-Lost Dutchman!" he says, turning his head from side to side like that's gonna stop the ants from crawling up there. "He's got a, a room at the Lost Dutchman! He's there now! Now make 'em stop. Pleeez, make 'em stop. Aaaaahhhhh!"

"All right," says Abel. "Now close your eyes as tight as you can." He uncorks the bottle of turpentine and starts pouring it on them, first on their heads, then over their feet, and then what was left over the rest of 'em. As he did this, the ants started falling off and curling up into little twitching balls. There was still a few holding on the way ants do, but the men were way beyond caring about one or two. They just sat there moaning and whimpering.

"Boyd, Lem," says Abel, "drag these two back over to the front of the house, get some water from the well, and douse them good. Then untie them, give them some food, and lock them up in the shed around back."

We did like Abel said, and when we got back around front, Abel was saddling up again.

"I'm going to the Lost Dutchman and end this," he says. "You better stay here with Dobbs until Slim gets back with the doctor."

"No way, Abel," says Lem. "We ain't lettin' you go down to the barn by yourself, let alone into town to face who knows how many of Randy's lackeys."

"Lem's right," I says. "Johnny and Bill can stay with Dobbs. You might be walking into a trap in town, or you might run into trouble on the road. Either way, you're gonna have some company."

"Fine, whatever you boys say," says Abel, sounding kinda tired. "Only first go back in there and tell those two not to leave Dobbsy alone, not with anyone."

So we told Bill and Johnny what to do and headed off for Gonzago for what seemed like the hundredth time. We didn't talk the whole way, and as we rode along I was thinking how being back in Gonzago was changing Abel. I mean, we got the information we wanted outta Fat Face and his companion, but torture just warn't the kinda thing Abel Braddock ever had to resort to before. It was justified and all, under the circumstances, and no permanent harm came to those men. But it was a sign that Abel was getting pushed too far, and I wondered what the hell was gonna happen next.

We didn't know how many men Randy still had on his side or what other schemes he had going, but I was hoping that once Randy himself was outta the way things would start getting back to normal, whatever that was. So much for worrying we was gonna be bored.

Well, when we got to town, we rode on past the Lost Dutchman without even looking at it and tied up in front of Wilson's like we was just there for a friendly drink. We went inside and sat down at the bar. Turns out Wendel was there with some of his friends, and they'd had a few, so wouldn't you know ol' Wendel comes staggering over to us, not knowing just how bad his timing was.

"Hey, Abe," he says, "we was just talking about you, weren't we boys? We wanna make sure you don't forget us when the time comes to take care of that murderin' bastard uncle of yers, you know, 'cause some of us have a score or two to settle with him and his gang a' wanted posters."

Meanwhile, over at his table of drinking pals, glasses were clinking together, and they was shouting, "Yeah!" and "Damn right!"

Abel didn't even turn around to look at Wendel, which, of course, Wendel found strange, him being a childhood pal and fulla whiskey.

"Hey, buddy," says Wendel, tapping Abel on the shoulder. "Whassa matter there? Didn't you hear me? I said—"

"He heard you, Wendel," says Lem, stepping in between 'em and putting his hand on Wendel's shoulder. "He's had a long day, and right now ain't a good time, so why don't you go back over to your table and have another round on me?"

"Hey, I was talking to my friend Abel Braddock, mister!" he says, pushing Lem's hand off his shoulder. "Me and him known each other longer'n you, so just back off!"

When his table fulla friends hears this, they stop toasting each other and put down their drinks, eyeing us like we just spoiled all their fun. Then Wendel starts pushing past me to get to Abel again, but I grabbed him by the shirt.

"C'mon, now, Wendel," I says, "let's keep this friendly, huh? Just leave him be." But Wendel wouldn't have none of that.

"Git yer hand offa me, boy!" he says. "You two ain't my friends, *he* is."

"All right, that's enough," says Abel, standing up and facing Wendel. "Wendel, I got some business to attend to right now, so do me a favor and go back over to your table."

Wendel looked like Abel'd just slapped him in the face, and he kinda staggered back a few steps.

"But Abe," he says, "I only wanted to tell ya I'm right behind ya when the time comes. You been away, but I'm telling ya that uncle a' yers been askin' for it."

"Just shut the hell up about him, will you?" says Abel in a loud voice. "My family's none of your goddamn business, so just keep your damn noses out of it, all of you! You hear? Not another word!"

Well, Wendel staggered back a little further, and suddenly the whole place was silent. Abel downed his shot of whiskey and started walking out.

"Let's go, fellers," he says, and me and Lem followed him to the door.

"I git it," says Wendel, loud so everyone can

hear. "You and yer soldier pals think yer too good fer us, is that it? Well, you ain't the only ones who fought in that war. I fought, n' so did Ralph there, and Caleb. Hell, this town's full of veterans. What makes you so special? You know what I think, boys? I think he's in it up to his neck with his precious uncle. Him, that quack of a doctor, and the rest of his mob, they're all in it. He never had any intention of payin' back Red for what he done 'cause now he's king of the hill, with a million-dollar ranch all ready for him when he comes strollin' back into town, the big hero. Well, your old man worked his fingers to the bone to build that ranch up from nothin' and make this town come alive, and folks around here ain't never gonna forget that. Never."

Abel was standing by the door listening to all this, and me and Lem figured any second he was gonna lay Wendel out. But he just stood there. Meanwhile, Wendel's pals were getting kinda nervous, and one of 'em got up and started towards him.

"Wendel," the feller says. "C'mon, now, leave him be. You had too much to drink."

"Shut up, Caleb," says Wendel, "I know what I'm doin'. I owe it to my old 'friend' here to let him know where the people of this town stand. When a man's father is murdered, he's supposed to avenge him, so if he don't, he's either a coward or he's mixed up in it himself. And everbody knows you ain't a coward, Abel. Get the picture?"

Abel walks slowly over to Wendel and stands right in front of him, looking him straight in the eye.

"I get it," says Abel, real calm again. "Is that all?"

"That about sums it up, yeah," says Wendel.

"Well, thanks for giving it to me straight," says Abel. "Be seeing ya."

9

So we left and started back up the street to the Lost Dutchman. But we'd only gone a few paces when there, in the middle of the street, was Randy, just standing there waiting. He was all alone, though you could see some rough looking characters lounging around in front of the Lost Dutchman who you just knew was working for Randy.

"Hold it right there, Braddock!" shouts Randy as we got to about fifty feet off. He had his holster on, and his arms was hanging in the air at his sides.

"Tell your help there to step aside," he says. "This is between you and me."

Abel nods at us, so me and Lem moved off to the left.

"Is Randy out of his ever-lovin' mind?" says Lem. "How could he be so stupid? If Doc Rivers couldn't get the job done, how's he gonna—somethin's screwy here."

I was thinking the same thing, that there was something underhanded going on, 'cause that was Randy's way. I looked over at Randy's scruffy gang again, but they was just hanging around with their hands in their pockets or their arms folded, and most of 'em looked like they warn't even carrying.

"Lem," I says nervously, "what are we forgetting here?"

"I don't know, I don't know," he says, his eyes darting all around trying to spot whatever Randy had up his sleeve. There warn't any guns poking outta windows that we could see and, except for them scruffy looking fellers, there warn't nobody else in the area. Just some folks way down the other end of town, too far away to pose any kinda threat.

"You ready, Braddock?" says Randy. He warn't drunk, neither, so unless he was committing suicide, he was up to something for sure.

"Ready when you are," says Abel, eyeing Randy with a little bit of a smile. If he suspected something was up, he warn't showing it.

"This is for my father, you rat!" shouts Randy as he goes to draw.

Like before, Abel's gun was out before Randy's hand was even on the butt of his pistol, but this time no shot rang out.

Abel was pulling the trigger, but his gun was just going click, click, click.

"I got you now, you bastard!" yells Randy, who starts aiming his gun with both hands.

"Shit!" says Lem, and we both draw on Randy. But the same thing happens to us—no bang, just click, click, click. Randy's gang is looking at us, and they start laughin' their heads off. We look over at Abel, who ain't panicking at all, but instead just lowers his gun hand and stands there, smiling and waiting for the bullet he knows is coming. Me and Lem start running towards Abel, but before we can get two steps, Randy fires. The bullet strikes Abel's left arm above the elbow, jerking him back slightly, but he just keeps standing there. When we hear the shot, me and Lem stop in our tracks, and we hear Randy say, "Aw, hell!" We start towards Abel again as Randy takes aim a second time, and another shot, much louder than the first, crackles through the air from someplace else. Nothing happens to Abel, but up the street we see Randy drop his gun and look down at a big red hole in his chest. Then he keels over backward, and finally, his boys, who was just standing there gaping like idiots, go running over to where he fell. Meanwhile, me and Lem go over to Abel to see if he's all right. The bullet musta hit a big vein, 'cause his arm was bleeding pretty bad, so I tore off a piece of my shirt and tied it around the arm above the wound.

"You okay?" asks Lem.

"Yeah, fine," he says, "thanks to Jimbo there."

We turn around to see Jimbo McCullock walking past the little crowd that was kneeling over Randy. Jimbo was carrying a double-barrel shotgun, which he was keeping at the ready in case any of Randy's boys tried anything. Just as well, 'cause we sure as hell couldn't cover him with what we was carrying.

"Jimbo," says a smiling Abel as the big feller saunters up. "Sure glad somebody around here had a loaded gun other than Randy there. He dead?"

"Yeah," says Jimbo. "Sorry I didn't get him before he got off that first round, but I only just heard what he was up to a few minutes ago and, since I don't carry myself, I had to run up the street and borrow this from a friend. I only meant to take out his gun hand, but I ain't such a good shot. Bet you wanted to finish him yourself."

"Doesn't matter to me," says Abel. "Just so the little cheat is in hell, where he belongs."

"Hold it right there, McCullock!" says a voice from behind us. It was Sheriff Wellman, holding a shotgun of his own. "Drop that thing, and pronto!"

"Anything you say, Sheriff," says Jimbo, placing the weapon on the ground. "There y'are."

"Hang on, Sheriff," says Abel. "Jimbo here just saved my life."

"Yeah, I know he did," says Wellman, putting his foot on the barrel of Jimbo's gun.

"Only there's a law against shooting people in the back like that. You know the rules, Abel. A fair fight's one thing, but I can't allow crap like that."

"Fair fight my ass," says Lem. "Someone pulled a switcheroo on us. Look." Lem takes Abel's gun and dumps out the bullets, twists one of 'em apart, and pours a little pile of sand into the palm of his hand. "See?" he says. "Some smart fuck even replaced the gunpowder with sand so we wouldn't notice the difference in weight."

"So someone switched your bullets," says Wellman. "So what? A dirty trick, all right, but what's that got to do with what Jimbo just pulled?"

"Whad'ya mean what's it got to do with it?" says Lem, raising his voice. "It's got everything to do with it. Who d'ya think switched them bullets, fairies?"

"Can you prove who switched 'em?" says the sheriff.

"I overheard two grimy looking guys up the street talking about it," says Jimbo.

"Oh, and I'm sure if we ever see those men again," says the sheriff, "they'll be only too happy to testify in court that they saw the bullets being switched. And I find it hard to believe you left your guns lying around for Randy or one of his men to mess with. Sorry, but I got to take you in, Jimbo. You can tell it to the judge."

"Now hold it," says Abel. "You're right. Randy never had access to our guns. But his sister did. It's the only possible explanation. I've got a man back at Elsinore who's on the brink of death after getting kidnapped, starved, and beaten on the orders of that piece of shit on the ground over there, and you know as well as I do he set up that little shoot-out with Doc Rivers. If Rivers had won and someone gave you proof that Randy paid him, you could've hanged both of them for murder. And his sister's been involved right from the get-go. So don't start throwing the law at me, Matt, or I'll start preferring charges myself."

"Go ahead, Abel, I'll even do what I can to help you," says Wellman, bending over to pick up Jimbo's shotgun. "But if I look the other way when bystanders get into the act every time two men want to shoot it out, there'd be mayhem around here. I'm not crazy about allowing these gunfights at all. If I could prevent them I would. But I got to draw the line somewhere, and Jimbo just stepped over it. Sorry."

"Don't worry, Abel, I'll be all right," says Jimbo as the sheriff led him away. "Besides, no matter what happens, it was worth it. But come by the jail later on and visit me. I got something important to discuss with you."

Well, it was looking like, other than us and Red, poor Jimbo was the only person in Gonzago Abel could trust, and now he was in the slammer. Abel felt so bad that he started going on about busting him out later that night, and me and Lem just barely talked him out of it by pointing out that we really oughta be heading back to Elsinore because Johnny and Bill prob'ly had their bullets switched, too. So we got back on our horses and started the ride back, but not before picking up a whole bunch of fresh bullets at the store on our way.

We hadn't even gotten outta sight of Gonzago when a group of men come burning the breeze the other way. We signal for them to stop and ask them where's the fire.

"The Comanches are on the warpath!" says one of 'em.

"What do you mean, 'on the warpath'?" says Abel.

"There's been a small wagon train attacked today, not more than fifteen miles from here," says another feller. "The savages killed every man, woman, and child. Made a real mess of 'em, too."

"How do you know it was Comanches?" asks Lem. "I mean, if they was all killed, who saw them?"

"What're you talkin' about, man?" says the same feller. "There's no mistakin' the work of them butchers! And scalpin' is the least of it. Oh, Lord, I hope I never see nothin' like that ever again."

"And besides," says the youngest of 'em, maybe fifteen, "the people we found had money, lots of it, and they left it lying around like it was nothing. Ever know a white or Mexican bandit who leaves money lying around like that? C'mon, we're wasting time talkin' here. You with us?"

"What do you mean, are we with you?" says Abel.

"We're rounding up the biggest posse this town's ever seen," says the youngster, "and we're gonna head out to that Comanche village and get some payback. Burn the place to the ground and wipe 'em out. Why don't you boys tag along? We sure could use you."

"Uh, I got to check and see if everything's all right at my ranch first," says Abel, obviously playing for time.

"Where's your ranch?" says junior.

"Elsinore," says Abel.

"Elsinore?" says one of the older fellers. "You Abel Braddock?"

"That's right," says Abel. "Why? Something happen over there?"

"Naw, the attack was well to the east of yer place, on the road to Redstone," he says. "But, hell, Mr. Braddock, havin' you head the posse would cinch it. Boys, meet Abel Braddock, Indian slayer. You all know his reputation for thinnin' out them herds of Sioux up north. He's a regular Davy Crockett, he is."

"Gee," says the young one. "I heard about you, Mr. Braddock. Now we'll really whip them Comanches good."

"It'd be an honor to fight alongside you, Mr. Braddock," says another one, and so on, down the line.

Abel musta been mighty uncomfortable with all that crap being thrown his way, but he didn't let it show. Instead he took advantage of what saps these fellers was.

"I'll be glad to lead the attack," says Abel, "but we can't just go rushing in there in force, not yet."

"Why can't we?" says the young one. "They're just gonna kill more innocent people if we wait."

"Because they've got scouts all over the place," says Abel, "and there wouldn't be a single trace of them by the time we got all the way to their village. They can ride twice as fast as we can."

Even though Abel had no intention of leading a posse of cretins—I learned that word from Dobbsy—all of what he was saying about the Comanches was true enough.

"So what'll we do, then?" says the one who compared Abel to Davy Crockett.

"You boys go on into town," says Abel, "and enlist as many men as you can, like you planned, only tell them to gather on Main Street tomorrow morning with their horses and guns ready. They're to wait until I send word what to do. If no word comes by three o'clock, they're to go home and reassemble there the following morning. Now, it's getting late and it's clouding up, so there'll be no moon tonight, which means there probably won't be any more attacks before tomorrow day, but between now and then I'd advise against traveling in groups of less than eight—let's make it ten. And remember, anyone who takes it upon himself to start this thing without first getting word from me or one of my men, I can guarantee he'll lose his own scalp and endanger all of us. I mean it."

The men, 'specially the youngster, was plainly disappointed they wasn't gonna see some action right away, but they agreed to follow Abel's instructions and rode off toward Gonzago. Meanwhile, we hit the trail again back to Elsinore.

"Well, that'll keep them out of trouble for a day or so," says Abel. "But we're gonna have to figure something out soon. After we get back and see how Dobbs is doing, I'd like to take a look at this so-called Comanche attack. I smell a rat."

"I don't know what you mean by that," I says, "but I can tell you right now that Many Horses and his warriors didn't have nothing to do with no massacre, not unless they was attacked first. He's a good man, that Many Horses. We told him to expect a visit from you, Abel. I think you're gonna like him."

"That'll be a nice change," says Abel. "And what I mean by smelling a rat is there's just been too much shit going on at once for it not to be connected in some way. Maybe Randy's last earthly act was to send some of his men out to stir up trouble at Many Horses' village. Anyway, let's hope he didn't start any other mischief in motion before he kicked off."

"Amen to that," says Lem. "You know, for a pea-brained coward who drank too much, that Randy sure had a lotta irons in the fire. But what about Daphne? I mean, she sure as hell ain't gonna come walkin' back into the house like nothin's happened. She musta gone somewhere."

"But not far enough away, I'm afraid," says Abel. "She's as looney as her brother was, so she's not about to give up and move on and start over fresh someplace else. Nope, she's still in the area waiting to pounce; the more so when she hears her little plan didn't work and her precious Randy's crossed the great divide ahead of schedule."

"If she's out *there*," I says, "them Comanches better watch out."

When we got back, Red was there with his doctor looking over Dobbsy while Johnny and Bill hovered in the background.

"Abel!" says Red as we walk in. "Jesus, your arm. Doc, have a look at that, will you?"

"Never mind me," says Abel, "what about Dobbs? Will he—"

"He'll make it," says the doctor, smiling as he starts undoing my makeshift bandage from Abel's arm. "I've given him something for the pain, but really all he needs is nourishment and sleep."

"All right, Abel," says Red, "now, what happened? Randy hire another gun?"

"Nope," says Abel, gritting his teeth as the

doctor dug into the wound to find the slug. "Randy himself."

"*Randy* did that?" says Bill. "He snuck up on you, right?"

"Not quite," says Abel. "Someone replaced my bullets this morning with duds. You and Johnny better check your ammo, too, because Boyd and Lem had the same problem. Which reminds me, Red, where did Daphne go this morning?"

"She said she was going to visit her cousins over in Buck's Creek and would probably stay the night," says Red. "I told her I didn't think this was any time to go calling, and—you mean . . . ?"

"I mean," says Abel, "I think you'll find she's not at her cousins' in Buck's Creek and that you're going to have to find someone else to mend your socks from now on. She's been playing us all for suckers the last few days. Hell, we're probably lucky to be alive, having her in the house all this time."

Johnny leans over to me and asks in a whisper why Red just don't have his maid mend his socks for him. Good ol' Johnny.

Meanwhile, Red, who was staring at Abel in disbelief for a while, leans back in his chair, shaking his head.

"And Randy?" he says finally.

"Dead," says Abel.

"Well, thank God for that at least," says Red, letting out a big sigh of relief.

"I don't get it," says Bill. "What'd you do, hit him over the head a few times with your gun after he shot you?"

"An old friend came to the rescue," says Abel. "And that's another problem we're going to have to solve." So then Abel explains about Jimbo being in jail, the Indian attacks, the posse, everything.

"Well, like I told you before," says Red, "Many Horses would never authorize an attack, especially not a massacre. But if those fools had gone off half-cocked to his village, they would've started a wholesale war."

"Yeah, I know," says Abel. "Bill here had a long conversation with Many Horses that leads me to suspect those attacks were faked to look like the work of Comanches on the warpath. Many Horses sounds like a smart man who'd do anything to keep the peace."

"Oh, so you've talked to Many Horses, then?" says Red.

"That's right," says Abel. "And Bill says he mentioned a couple of run-ins with some men from Elsinore who tried to intimidate him into selling some Comanche land."

Red stood up and raised his arms like he was giving up on everything.

"I knew it!" he says. "Randy was hiring my own fucking men behind my back! I must be the all-time idiot! First I go and hire all that rabble—"

"Red, you had a ranch to run," says Abel,

"and you needed bodies. You can blame the town of Gonzago for making it a crime around here to work for you."

"Aw, screw that!" says Red. "I should've let the stupid ranch go to hell in a handbasket before I hired a single outlaw! They turned out to be next to useless anyway. The place is falling apart as we speak, so what did I accomplish? Huh? You tell me, what did I gain? I'll tell you what, a goddamn war with the Comanches, that's what! Not to mention almost getting you and your men killed."

"Before you start assuming there's a war on," says Abel, "let me check out one of the attack sites first thing tomorrow to see if it really was Comanches or some of Randy's crew trying to get everyone to think Many Horses has dug up the old hatchet."

"That could be, I suppose," says Red, calming down a bit. "With everything the Eckhardts have pulled lately, I guess you can't put anything past them. But, my God, slaughtering innocent people like that? Women and children?"

Red put his head down on the table and started sobbing.

"What kind of monsters have I been sharing my house with?" he says. "If I hadn't stepped in, played the guardian angel for those animals all these years, none of this would've happened. Those children would still be alive, their mothers—"

"Red," says Abel. "What's done is done.

Right now we've got to concentrate on keeping things from getting any worse."

But Red wouldn't listen. He just kept crying and cursing away.

"That bitch!" says Red, practically spitting the words out.

"She better be a hundred miles away by now, 'cause if I ever get my hands on her, I swear, I'll put out those baby blue eyes of hers with my goddamn finger. I will! I'll do it!"

"Come on, boys," says Abel. "Let's hit the sack so we can get another early start. After we take a look at the massacre site, we've got to go talk to Many Horses, then go back into town and break up that mob. Plus I've got to see Jimbo and find out what's so important, so it's going to be a long day. Whoever's up first, wake me. Red—"

But Red was off in his own world, either not hearing or not listening. So Abel just pats him on the back and we all left the room.

As I lay in bed trying to sleep, I didn't know who I oughta feel sorrier for, Abel or Red. Both of 'em was having all their dreams come crashing down around them, but I guess Red was worse off on account of how he was older and didn't have nothing left to look forward to, really. He prob'ly had got used to everyone in town hating him and thinking he was a murderer, but now he really did have some dead people on his conscience. Even though them getting killed warn't really his fault, I reckon if I was in his shoes I'da felt the same. A man's gotta live with the decisions he makes, and Red just kept making one bad one after another. I got to thinking Red wouldn't be long for this world, that one way or another he was on his way out.

10

We was all up and on the road before sunrise, all except for Johnny, who was staying behind to watch Dobbsy, and Red, who wouldn'ta been no good to us anyhow. It took us awhile to reach the spot where the wagon train was ambushed, but it only took us a few minutes to figure out that it warn't no Comanche attack.

We had to shoo off some big vultures that was having quite a feast for themselves when we arrived, and Abel shot one that was working on what was left of a poor little girl. Even so, we had to keep scaring them off 'cause they kept coming back for more while we was there. You couldn't hardly tell the men from the women on account of they was so badly sliced up.

The horses was gone, like you'd expect in an Indian raid, and, apart from being mutilated, the bodies was all scalped. But you could tell right away that whoever scalped 'em didn't know what they was doin'. And the other thing that gave it away was the money that was scattered all over, like that poor excuse for a lynch mob said it was. But there was too much of it for them folks that was laying there to be carrying. They was poor people—you could tell from their clothes and the wagons. And even if they coulda had all that money, you just knowed it was planted by someone, a little here, a little there, every damn where, in fact.

That kinda stupid, obvious crap could only be the work of the dumb bastards Randy'd been using, or fellers like 'em. But, as dumb as they was, they was also a bunch of heartless killers who we all decided right then we was gonna hunt down and finish off ourselves when the time come.

"I've seen enough," says Abel. "Take out your shovels and let's dig these poor people a temporary grave until we can have the bodies moved to the town cemetery."

So we dug a big, shallow hole and laid the bodies in it—fourteen of 'em—then covered 'em up with dirt so the vultures couldn't get at 'em no more. It was pretty grim work, I'll tell you that, and that's coming from someone who saw hundreds of men fall in battle and thousands more dead bodies laying around, some of 'em fresh and some skeletons and some in between. It warn't even that there was women and children in there,

though that was pretty hard to take; it was knowing why they was killed and who done it that
gave us all a knot in the pit of the stomach as we
covered 'em up.

Our next stop was the Comanche village, but
when we got to that small ridge we was at before
and looked down, we couldn't see nothing but a
big, empty clearing.

"You sure this is the spot?" says Abel,
knowing damn well we don't make mistakes like
that.

"Look, you can tell there was a camp in that
clearing down there," says Bill. "They just up
and left. We can follow the trail easy enough,
with all those horses and poles scraping along
behind, but—"

"Yeah," says Abel, "their rearguard scouts
wouldn't let us get within a mile of their new
camp. Goddamn it, I can't believe those morons
went ahead and started something already."

"It's possible they moved as a precaution,"
says Bill. "I mean, if Many Horses' scouts caught
wind of that staged massacre back there,
wouldn't they move anyway, before the whites
could mount any kind of large-scale attack? I sure
as hell would."

"Good point, Bill," says Abel. "Let's take a
quick look around for any signs of action."

So we scoured the area, but didn't find no
cartridges or prints that'd show a fight took
place, just the marks you usually find after a
tribe of Indians breaks camp. They done a fair

job of covering their tracks and the ruts their travois poles made—prob'ly good enough to fool those idiots back in Gonzago, but not good enough to keep *us* from finding them if and when the time comes. I was kinda hoping we would meet up with Many Horses again 'cause he really interested me. But, for now, we was gonna pound leather back into Gonzago to see what them chuckle-headed townsfolk was up to.

When we got into Gonzago, it was still morning, but the posse was there already, in force and gathered round in a big circle. When a couple of 'em spied Abel riding up, they got all frantic and noisy about it.

"Here he comes, boys!" shouts one of 'em, and a big cheer goes up.

As we approached the circle, we could see there was something goin' on in the center of it all. As Abel dismounted, the circle parted for him, and there in the middle we see they had got a big Comanche warrior tied up. They had him laying on the ground, and the mob kicked him and spit on him and called him all sorts of names, but he just lay there, not reacting in any way, just staring straight ahead. Right away, I recognized him as one of Many Horses' men, the one who pulled back the flap of his teepee.

"What the hell is going on here?" yells Abel, running up and standing over the Comanche so they couldn't kick the poor feller without going through him first. "Just what in hell do you think you're doing? Are you out of your minds?"

The crowd hushed up real fast, and the faces went from wide-eyed grinning to slack-jawed confusion.

"Didn't I tell you men not to do anything without hearing from me first?" shouts Abel. "Do you idiots have any idea what you've done?"

"Now hang on a minute, there, Mr. Braddock," says one of the men from that group we run into the day before. "We caught this here Injun dead to rights."

"What are you talking about?" says Abel.

"I'm talkin' about there was another attack this mornin'," he says, "over at the Miller's place. Old man Miller and his wife was killed, cut to pieces like them poor folks was yesterday, and their horses taken. Their stable boy got away and run next door and told Bill Kearny here. So Bill got his boys and—you tell him, Bill."

This big, barrel-chested feller steps forward, real defiant, and finishes the story.

"My boys and me got our rifles and rode around the area and we found this one," he says, jerking his thumb in the direction of the Comanche, "skulkin' around nearby. My oldest shot his horse out from under him, and we chased him down and roped him. Look, mister, I don't know what's eatin' you, but maybe you better go on out to the Miller place and take a good look for yourself at what deviltry was done out there. If you still gotta problem, then we don't want your help leadin' no posse against them bastards."

"I already saw what happened out on the road to Redstone," says Abel, "and it ain't Comanches. The vermin that killed all those people are as white as you and me."

An angry murmur went through the crowd when Abel says this.

"What?" yells Kearny. "That's about the dumbest thing I ever heard. There's Indian pony tracks all over the place, scalps taken, horses stolen, and then this feller here nosin' around. What more do you want?"

"I know what it looks like," says Abel, "but trust me, it's all a big con job by someone who wants us at war with the Comanches."

"All right," says Kearny. "I've had about all I can take. This is sheer foolery, standin' around listenin' to the big Indian expert here. Forgettin' for a minute how damn ridiculous it'd be for us to believe some of our own done that to the Millers and them settlers, what's so crazy about the notion that the Comanches around here are on the warpath? Just because they ain't pulled anything in a couple years? Hell, a hundred miles east of here it's been open season on white settlers since Texas got civilized. And the locals? If you ask me, they been long overdue for a while now."

Kearny was winning the mob over. They started going, "Yeah!" and "That's right!" and "You tell 'em, Bill!"

"I'm not going to stand here and argue with you," says Abel, starting to lose his patience. "Untie that warrior and let me escort him back to his people, and just maybe I can stop them from really going on the warpath and turning Gonzago into a ghost town."

"They're already on it, you fool," says Kearny. "If we done like you say and you took this savage back to his village, all you'd get out of it is some ventilation on the top of your thick head. You think these Indians'd be grateful to you for settin' one of their own free? They ain't like us, Braddock. They'd skin you alive, and probably him along with you for gettin' himself caught."

"Now who's playing the Indian expert?" says Abel. "You ever spend any time fighting them?"

Kearny steps forward a few feet and eyes Abel with contempt.

"No, *Colonel*," he says, "can't say as I did. See, I never had time to go off adventurin' like you. I was too busy raisin' my younger brothers and sisters after some of your precious Comanches killed my ma and pa. They weren't trespassin' on Indian land or nothin', just on their way back from town. They slit their throats for a broken-down old nag and a sackful of sugar. What more do I need to know about 'em, other than that they're murderin' scum?"

Well, that really got the crowd worked up, and suddenly we found the circle of angry men was starting to close in around us.

"Look, Kearny," says Abel. "I'm sorry about your folks, but that happened a long time ago, before there were any treaties or anything. And I admit that even now there's still plenty of hostile groups scattered around Texas. But the tribe in our area happens to be peaceful, and all I'm trying to do is see that it stays that way. You're just going to have to trust me about these attacks. At least let me try."

It didn't look good. Judging from his face, Kearny warn't backing down, and everyone else in that mob looked like their minds was made up.

"No deal, Braddock," he says finally. "You can go and get yourself killed, for all I care, but this Comanche's all ours, and after we settle his hash, we're gettin' that posse together and track down every last one of 'em. They broke treaty first, so the Union army people won't have nothin' to say about it.

"You're out of your heads if you think an untrained, disorganized gang of angry men can take on that tribe and win," says Abel. "Even if you had even numbers, they'd cut you down in a matter of minutes. But the fact is there're two, maybe three times as many of them as there are of you. And how many of you are crack shots? Huh? Be honest with yourselves, now, 'cause you're all about to make a decision that's gonna mean the difference between being alive or dead at the end of the day."

Now some of the men in the crowd was looking a little unsure, going from holding their rifles out in front of 'em with both hands to holding them by the barrel with one hand and the butt resting on the ground at their sides. It warn't much, but it showed they was starting to think the thing through a bit, and probably more than a few of 'em was already picturing themselves on the business end of a Comanche lance.

"And how many of you men have wives and families depending on you?" says Abel. "Can you really afford to take the risk that by tonight they'll be all alone in this world? And let me ask you this: If you start this thing and lose, which means every one of you is dead, 'cause the Comanches don't take prisoners, what's going to stop them from sweeping down on your farms and ranches and houses and wiping out your loved ones? Think about it, men. There's a full moon tonight and not a cloud in the sky."

Well, it was really starting to work now, 'cause more'n half the mob was talking among themselves and shifting their weight from one foot to the other and in general just looking for any excuse to hightail it on home right then and there so they could hug their wives, sit their kids on their knees, and let the ol' gun go to rust in the shed.

"Sorry, Bill," says one feller as he walks past Kearny, "but I'm out."

"Me, too," says another feller.

And then the floodgate opened. In a coupla minutes, there warn't more'n a dozen men left on Main Street of the original mob of thirty or forty.

"That was real clever, Braddock," says Kearny with a sneer. "But there's still enough of us to make trouble for them butchers, and in any case we ain't lettin' this one go no matter what you say."

"Are the rest of you men ready to die because of Bill Kearny's grudge?" says Abel.

"Forget it, Braddock," says Kearny. "You weeded out all the sissys for me. These fellers don't scare so easy."

"I'm asking *them*," says Abel. "Well?"

One of the die-hards steps forward, giving Abel a sympathetic look.

"Listen, Braddock," he says, "I ain't got no beef with you, and I ain't in this 'cause of Bill. I saw the bodies out there on the side of the road. I saw them kids. I ain't got no kids of my own, but it ain't right for them to hafta die like they did. Now, to me it look like the work of Comanches, but you say it ain't, and you been around Indians. I'd like to believe you, I really would—I may not be no fam'ly man, but I ain't in no hurry to die neither. But how do you explain this here feller bein' caught near the Miller's if he ain't got nothin' to do with it?"

"To be honest," says Abel, "I can't explain it.

But I do know that killing him's not gonna solve anything. If I was sure the Comanches were already on the warpath and that this warrior was one of the one's who murdered the Millers, I'd say go ahead, do what you want with him. But I'm convinced this is all a big setup, and by killing this man you'll be playing right into the hands of whoever's behind it."

"Yeah, I know," says the other feller. "But if you're wrong and we let him go, that's one more of them to fight against us. Sorry, Braddock, but I say he stays."

"I agree," says another feller. "We all agree, or we wouldn't still be standing here."

So, that was it. If we was gonna set that Comanche free, the four of us was gonna have to take on twelve to do it. Abel stood there sizing up the situation, and I'm sure the thing going through his head right then was how we could do it without having to shoot any of 'em. After all, they couldn't be blamed for thinking the Comanches really were on the warpath.

Then a crazy thing happened. All this time, that Comanche was just laying there on the ground behind Abel, not struggling or moving or even making a face. Then all of a sudden, he lifts himself up and grabs Abel's gun right out of the holster even though his hands was tied together at the wrist. Then he rolls over and aims the gun right up at Abel—the one man who's trying to save his life. So me, Lem, and Bill all opened up on him at once, emptying our guns into him on account of he's an Indian, and a tough one at that.

The rest of the crowd was so surprised that none of 'em even raised a weapon. Yeah, I thought, they woulda been real handy in an all-out fight with the Comanches. But soon as the firing stopped, they all recovered their wits sufficient to start telling Abel they told him so.

"I guess *that'll* learn ya," says one really dumb looking feller. I wanted to punch him right in the nose.

"See?" says another one. "They don't care about no treaty."

"Yeah," says his friend next to him. "They ain't like reg'lar people, more like a caged animal. Bite the hand that feeds ya right off if ya let 'em."

Poor Abel just stood there for a minute, wondering what went wrong. But he snaps out of it quick enough.

"Come on," he says, picking up his gun and jumping back on his horse. "Let's go."

"What about Jimbo?" says Lem as we start riding past the jail.

"That'll have to wait," says Abel. "Right now we gotta find Many Horses and try to sort this mess out before those men can start anything."

No one wanted to ask, but Bill finally got the nerve up.

"So, Abel," he says. "What just happened back there?"

Abel smiled.

"You mean," he says, "why did he try to shoot me instead of one of the others? I don't know. I suppose the most logical explanation is that he simply didn't understand English. I mean, he certainly had a reason to grab the gun and start shooting after being captured and kicked around like that. How was he supposed to know I was trying to help him?"

"Because he must've recognized us from our little visit to his village," says Bill, "and you were obviously our friend."

"Maybe he was so confused he didn't recognize you," says Abel. "I don't know."

Abel had a point, but Bill had a better one, and Abel knowed it. Whatever the answer was, we was sure gonna try and find out.

We got back to where the Comanche camp had been and started following their trail. We could've used Johnny, but there was no time to go back to Elsinore now, not until we located Many Horses.

After about an hour, the trail we was following just kinda disappeared on us. They musta started carrying everthing by hand and strapped across their horses instead of dragging it all behind. We was able to pick up small traces for a few hundred yards further, but then even those dried up and we was stumped.

We stopped and was discussing maybe sending one of us back for Johnny when a Comanche warrior appears up ahead and beckons us to follow him. He leads us on for a ways, and then we notice there's another warrior behind us, about a hundred yards back.

"Not takin' any chances, are they?" says Lem.

"That one back there's probably covering up any trail we might've left," says Abel. "Smart."

So, finally, after another half-hour of traveling, we come over a rise and see the village, looking exactly the way it looked in the other place. As we're approaching, a bunch of warriors ride up to us and point to our guns, so we hand 'em over. Then they stop our horses and make us get off and walk the rest of the way. Many Horses was standing in front of his teepee, looking even more serious than he did before, if that's possible.

"You take a very great chance in coming here," says Many Horses looking at Bill. "And we take an even greater one letting you find us. There will not be peace between us for much longer, gentlemen, so this will be the last time such a meeting will be possible."

Bill steps forward and pulls Abel with him.

"Many Horses," he says, "this is the man I spoke of, Abel Braddock. He will find a way to keep peace."

Many Horses looked Abel up and down and then put out his hand.

"Abel Braddock," he says, "your friends have told me you are an honest and brave man, and were this another time, I would be eager to spend time with you and your friends, to talk and teach each other what we know. But I fear it is now too late, even for such a man as yourself, to stop what has already begun. My people are afraid and my warriors are restless, and I myself am no longer certain that I want peace."

"Many Horses," says Abel, "I know that you must be a man of peace. If not, the last five years would not have been possible."

"It is true that I desire peace," says Many Horses, "but only because I know it is the only way for my people to survive. We are a warrior people at heart, and I was once a great and fearless warrior myself. I am not ashamed to tell you, because it was a different time and I was a young man seeking to prove himself on the field of battle like all young men of my tribe, but once I killed many of your people and took great pleasure in it. But, as you see, I am now an old man, and even the bravest of men becomes cowardly as he grow old, asking only of life that he be permitted to live another day. You are still quite young, but you will see."

"Sometimes, Many Horses," says Abel, "it is better to be wise than brave. The Comanche tribes to the east are led by brave men, but they do not counsel wisely by urging war, because soon the United States government will force them all off their lands. So, you see, bravery without wisdom has no value."

Many Horses broke into a smile, prob'ly the first one in a long, long while.

"Perhaps," he says. "And yet, wisdom cannot always prevail. I am beginning to think I owe my people the chance to meet a brave end rather than peacefully surrendering to the will of the white man. I am not sure."

"I understand, Many Horses," says Abel. "When that day comes, that's a decision you'll have to make. You and your people still have time—more than your cousins to the east, anyway."

"You are wrong," says Many Horses. The smile was gone. "I know why you are here; you wish to warn me that some of your people will soon attack us. And when they do, we will defend ourselves. But the Great Father in Washington will not care that we did not begin the fighting, only that the treaty has been broken. So you see, you have wasted your time coming here."

"Then you know about the attacks of the last two days?" says Abel.

"Of course," says Many Horses. "I have eyes and ears all over this area. At first, when my scouts told me the white men were killing their own people, females and children, I did not understand. Then I realized what it meant. I suppose it is really a very clever trick, but it is the kind of trick that only a white man could have thought of. To me, it is a terrible thing for any man to do, cowardly and low. These men wish to push us off the land, but they will not come and fight us. Instead they incite others to do their fighting for them, and these others we will be forced to kill. No, with such men in the world, we cannot last."

"Many Horses," says Abel, "the men who want you off the land, tell me about them. You said they are from my ranch, is that right?"

"Yes," says Many Horses. "You see, Abel Braddock, if even you and your friends cannot discover them, working amongst you on your own ranch, then how can we hope to defeat them?"

"We'll see about that," says Abel. "What do they look like?"

"I cannot say; they cover their faces," says Many Horses.

"Tell me, Many Horses," says Abel, lookin' thoughtful, "have any of your warriors disappeared from or left the tribe for any reason in the past year or so?" says Abel.

"Only yesterday. One of my scouts was taken by a group of white men near the place of one of the attacks," says Many Horses. "I know they will kill him because they will assume he was responsible. But I do not mourn for him, because he was one of the restless warriors I spoke of. He wished for war between our two peoples so he could meet a brave death, and I have no doubt that he has gotten his wish by now."

"You are right, Many Horses," says Bill. "He met a brave death. We, we saw it happen."

Well, none of us had the nerve to tell Many Horses that we was the ones who killed him.

Even though we didn't have no choice and all, we just couldn't tell him.

"Have any other warriors disappeared?" says Abel.

"Yes, one other," says Many Horses, looking away like he was ashamed. "One who was to die escaped."

"Why was he to die?" says Abel.

"For stealing," he says. "From the Sacred Place."

"What is this Sacred Place, Many Horses?" says Abel.

"As I have told your friends," he says, "it is a place known to my people for generations. Every warrior is taken there once, but no one is permitted to return there or to disturb it in any way. The warrior I speak of, Grey Sky, the one who was banished, went back to the Sacred Place and stole from it."

"And do you know where Grey Sky is now?" says Abel.

"No," says Many Horses. "Why do you ask of him?"

"Boyd, the coin," says Abel. I fished it out and tossed it over. This time, I knowed I warn't getting it back. But with all that was going on, I didn't much care.

Abel hands the coin over to Many Horses, who stares down at it, real sad.

"Where did you find this?" he says.

"It was on your warrior," says Abel. "He was with some white men who tried to ambush us when we first arrived. Many Horses, will you show me the Sacred Place? You have my word I will never reveal its location or tell anyone that it even exists."

Many Horses closed his eyes for a second.

"It is no longer a secret," he says. "The men with the long guns from your ranch, they already know where it is and what it is. Grey Sky betrayed us, as I feared one day one of our people would. I will show you."

11

Many Horses starts shouting orders to his warriors, who bring our horses over, and off we went
with Many Horses and about twenty warriors. We
rode north for about an hour, until we came to
the entrance to a little box canyon. We noticed
there was other warriors around the rim of the
canyon—sentries, I reckon—and then, inside the
canyon itself there was another twenty or so warriors waiting for us.

Many Horses took the lead, and we followed
him into the back end of the canyon. When we
got there, Many Horses dismounted and started
on foot up a narrow ledge that went up along the
canyon wall and disappeared behind some rocks
above. It was pretty steep, and the footing warn't
very good, but Many Horses was nimble as a cat,
taking long strides and jumping over rocks that
was in the way, while we just barely kept up.

About halfway up the canyon wall, the ledge ended at the mouth of a cave, and Many Horses led us inside. At first, it was too dark to see, but then, up ahead, we could see a hole was letting in a big shaft of sunlight. We got to where the light was, and there, scattered all around, was more gold than I ever seen in one place.

"Holy shit, would ya lookit that!" says Lem in a loud whisper.

It was them gold coins like my lucky piece, spilling out of a big ol' chest that was busted open and lying on its side. Then, as my eyes got used to the surrounding dark, I notice the skeletons. There was five of 'em propped up against the cave wall, grinning up at us. They was still wearing some kind of armor, with big round shoulders and chest plates and these funny looking steel hats that was round on the top and come to a point in the front and back.

"So this is what it's all about," says Abel. "A fortune in Spanish gold."

"Yes, Abel Braddock," says Many Horses. "These men you see here brought their gold with them from across the sea many years ago. No one knows why they came here. The legend that has been passed down to me says only that there was a great battle nearby with an army of these men which my people won. All of the invaders were killed, except for these five, who managed to escape the slaughter. But, as you see, they did not get very far, taking refuge here from those of my people who searched for them.

"By the time they were found, they were already dead from hunger and thirst. When my people saw the gold they carried, they were very excited and curious. It shone like the sun, and the invaders had guarded it so jealously that it cost them their lives. They might easily have escaped had they not been weighed down with the box of gold. Therefore, my people reasoned, it must be a very important thing, the source of powerful medicine, and they captured it. So, over the years, it became a symbol of my people's power, and the legend grew, as legends will with the passing of time.

"When I was a young man, my father brought me here and showed it to me, and later I showed my son. When my people would win a fight with the white settlers, who had better weapons and greater numbers, we felt we must have drawn the strength to do this from the Sacred Gold.

"But then I met a white man who came alone to this area, and we became good friends. His name was Matthew Cooper, and he came from the eastern place you call Kentucky. He was a great hunter, and was as good on a horse as the best of my tribe, but he was also a man of great learning. He taught me to speak your language quite well. He asked me about the Sacred Place, and I brought him here to show him, against the rules of our tribe.

"When he saw the gold and these men, he laughed. I asked him why, and he told me that this gold was indeed very powerful, but only among white men, who valued it above all else. He said that, one day, when the white men came to this area in great numbers, they would find out about the gold and try to steal it from us. I was outraged at the thought that men would try to take from us the source of our strength, and I said so. Then he told me that I should not allow my people to think they owe their strength to the gold, that they should be told it comes instead from a place inside themselves, something that no one can steal away because it cannot be seen or touched.

"But he also told me that, one day, the gold could be of great value to my people, and that we should continue to think of it as a sacred place and guard it. I asked him in what way would it be of value, but all he would say is that when the time came I would know. And now that the white man comes this way in great numbers, taking the land for his own use, I can see what my friend Matthew Cooper meant. He did not tell me then because he knew it would cause me great pain to hear that eventually my people would have to fight just to be allowed to stay here.

"One day soon, I will use that gold to do that strangest of all things the white man does: to buy land. It is the only way my people will be allowed to stay here.

"So over the years I have taught my people as my great friend told me to, and now this place is known only as the Sacred Place, but none of my people—except for me—knows why it is so special. They know only that it's very important and must be guarded at all times. Even Grey Sky, who stole some of the gold, had no idea of its value to the white men when he took it. He was merely a weak man. You see, even a proud and fierce people like ours has its weak men. So now you know, Abel Braddock, why I cannot allow the gold to be taken from us."

Well, that was quite a story, and I thought about that Matthew Cooper feller some. We was all quiet for a spell.

"Many Horses," says Abel finally, "I will help you and your people to keep their land."

"It is not *our* land," says Many Horses with a frown. Then he starts smiling again. "I am sorry. I know that is how the white man thinks, Abel Braddock, even good and brave white men like you and your friends. I welcome your help."

So we left the Sacred Place canyon and headed back toward Many Horses' village.

"Many Horses," says Abel once we was on our way, "the men who cover their faces, is there nothing you can remember about them that would help us find out who they are?"

"Let me see," says Many Horses, putting his fist up to his forehead. "Yes, the one who did the talking has bad lungs. He coughed whenever he spoke."

The four of us looked at each other. It was Slim.

"Well, that ties it," says Lem. "I thought he was actin' a little cagey."

"You know this man?" says Many Horses. "A friend of yours?"

"Not a friend," says Abel, "but we know him. He's my uncle's foreman. Jesus!"

Abel turned around and looked in the direction of Elsinore for a second. We was all thinking the same thing, that Slim being involved could only mean Red himself was calling the shots. 'Course, the real kicker was, it meant that snake'd been behind all the crap from the very start, that every single thing outta his mouth since we got here was a dirty lie. That he was in cahoots with Randy and Daphne. That he had that bloody scarf planted on the trail knowing we'd find it. That he was a cold-blooded murderer many times over. Hell, it probably meant he did kill Abel's father after all. And if that was the case, then it also meant Red's doctor was in on it—and right now he was looking after Dobbsy.

"Many Horses," says Abel, all outta breath, "we have to get back to the ranch as soon as we can. Our friends there are in great danger. But I promise to return soon and help you. And remember, you should expect some kind of attack very soon."

"Go to your friends, Abel Braddock," says Many Horses. "We will know they are coming long before they arrive. I wish you luck."

"Same to you," says Abel with a wave. Then we took off, burnin' the ol' breeze again, just hoping Johnny and Dobbs was still alive.

On the way back, all I could do was think about all the bullshit yarns we'd been fed since we got to Gonzago. It was really a kinda strange feeling, like we all just woke up from a long dream, the kind that don't make no sense, and now we was just trying to get our heads clear.

As we got about five miles off from the entrance to the ranch, we see up ahead what looked like that damn posse of fools, coming the other way at full gallop. There was about twenty-five of 'em. I guess some of 'em went and got liquored up after they quit and changed their minds again.

Well, I thought, that'd be their last drink. Many Horses had himself about eighty warriors to fight with, not including the ones guarding the Sacred Place. Their advance scouts would pro'bly have no trouble picking off this scruffy mob before they even left the main road. They was idiots, all right, but you still felt kinda bad for 'em.

"Hey, Abel!" shouts Bill over the pounding of our horses' hooves, "shouldn't we try one more time to turn those imbeciles back? Like Many Horses said, Washington's not going to care who started it."

"All right!" Abel yells back. "I'll give it another shot. But they better make up their minds in a hurry."

So we all pulled up and waited for the posse to come to us. There was definitely some poor riders in that bunch, and soused on top of it, 'cause even though the lead man signaled for them all to stop, half of 'em ended up fifty yards past us before their horses pulled up. Abel dismounts and walks up to Bill Kearny.

"What, you just come from warnin' your Comanche pals out there, Braddock?" he says.

"Kearny, you're leading these men to certain death," says Abel. "It was certain when you had twice this many; now you're gonna make it easy for them."

"We don't care if we don't make it back, Braddock!" shouts one feller. "We got a score to settle, n' you ain't gonna talk us outta goin' thish time!"

"Nice going, Kearny," says Abel. "Drinks were on you, huh? Look at this guy. He's so drunk he's falling off his saddle. And that one, too."

"We ain't *all* drunk," says another feller in the back.

"Please, boys," says Abel. "Just listen to me for one minute, just one, then you can go. Agreed? Bill?"

Kearny was about to say something, but when Abel calls him Bill, he stopped.

"Go ahead, Braddock," says Kearny, "for all the good it'll do you."

"Thanks, Bill," says Abel. "Look, right now I'm on my way back to Elsinore to have it out with my Uncle Red. I just found out that Red's behind those massacres."

"Here he goes again," says Kearny, rolling his eyes.

"Let me finish, Bill," says Abel, not looking over at Kearny. "I've also learned that Red had my father poisoned."

"Yeah, we heard that, too!" shouts one of the drunker fellers.

"As you all know," says Abel, "Red's gone and surrounded himself with a whole bunch of riffraff, who are at the ranch now, probably waiting for me. As you can see, there's only four of us. I could really use your help, all of you. Now, I've got to go *now*—the lives of two of my friends depend on it—so I can't spend any more time trying to convince you. But if you come with me now and help me get that bastard Red and his gang, I'll be able to prove to you that he's the butcher of those innocent women and children. Well, Bill? How about it?"

Kearny kinda looks down at the ground for a second, then over at Abel.

"All right, Braddock," he says, "we'll help you, for your old man's sake. But you better be right about Red."

Well, as excited as them fellers mighta been

at the prospect of taking on the cream of the
Comanche crop, they sounded twice as glad to be
let off the hook, hooting and yelling and slapping
each other on the back. Now they was gonna take
on some easier game, and that it was the much-
hated Red and his gang made it that much
sweeter.

"Let's go, boys!" shouts Kearny, and the
whole pack of us was off.

A couple lookouts for Red who was sitting
around in front of the gate to Elsinore nearly
jumped outta their skins when they seen us
coming. They barely had time to untie their
horses and mount up when we come roaring up
behind 'em. Kearny makes a gesture to two of
his men, who pull up alongside the lookouts and
jump right onto their backs at full speed. They
musta been two of the drunker ones to pull a
stunt like that, and I wondered if the men they
jumped on got hurt any worse than they surely
did. But we didn't have time to stop and see, so I
figured just as well to keep the drunk ones outta
the shooting that was gonna start up when we
got there.

As we got to the house, everything looked
real quiet. There wasn't a man or horse in sight.
Lem and me jump off our horses and go to open
the front door, but Abel grabs us from behind and
pulls us back.

"Something's going on," says Abel. "Johnny
would've come out as soon as he heard us ride
up." That didn't sound so good.

"Hey, Johnny!" shouts Abel. "Dobbs? Anybody home?"

Nothing. Then, all of sudden, there's bullets flying all over the place.

"Goddamn it!" shouts one of Kearny's boys, who got hit. Another one falls in the dirt and starts rolling around, clutching his belly. Everyone else runs for cover, most of 'em behind the woodpile, and a couple to the side of the barn.

Me, Abel, and Lem use our horses for cover—poor critters—and make it to the back of the house, where there's no windows, our backs flat against the wall. Our horses go galloping off as quick as they can, whinnyin' and snortin' their disapproval of how we just handled things. But Lem and me managed to pull our rifles out before they run off.

"Now what?" says Lem.

"All right," says Abel. "You two are gonna have to make a run for those trees over there." He was pointing to a little group of young oaks about forty feet from the side of the house hardly big enough to hide behind. "You're going to have to take out a couple of them before we can risk storming the house. I'll try to signal Bill or Kearny over there to do the same thing around front. Okay, go!"

I really hated having to expose my back to fire like that. Somehow, I didn't mind nearly as much running head-on into enemy guns. But we couldn't just stand there, huffing and puffing all day, so off we went, zigzagging as much as we could, dropping to the ground and rolling the last few feet. Fortunately for us, the quality of help Red hired was lousy all the way, so we got to the trees in one piece and made them use up a lot of ammunition trying to hit us, too. Once we was there, though, the poor cover them trees gave us become real obvious, so we had to work fast.

"Pick a window," says Lem.

"All the way on the right—the kitchen," I says.

I got one as soon as I drew a bead. The fool was all nicely lit up from behind, so I was even able to get a head shot, which was always desirable on account of how you knew you'd never have to bother with *that* feller ever again. Then they wised up in there and started drawing curtains and closing doors. But I just took aim at the center of the window, waited for the muzzle flash, adjusted my aim, and fired, hoping that the other feller's shot would be wide and mine wouldn't. Meanwhile, Lem was having some success also, and some firing started up around front, and then from the other side of the house.

After about ten minutes, the shooting died down to the occasional bang, and then, finally, all was quiet. 'Course, it mighta meant they was outta ammo or taking a rest, but with all the guns we had fixed on the place, it more likely meant they was all dead or wounded.

Abel signaled to us to hold our fire, and crawled around to the front door. We zigzagged on over to join him, and after all the men we had left was assembled behind Abel, he opens the door and we all rush in, pistols out.

Inside the door to the kitchen was three fellers, dead or dying, laying in a heap next to my window. Usually, I don't take pride in that sorta job, but it was all right this time 'cause of all the trouble they caused us and 'cause they was every last one of 'em a criminal wanted by the law in some state or other.

As we moved through the house, we found more of the same. Then we got to the room where we left Dobbsy. The door was closed, and when we opened it, we saw the worst sight we coulda hoped for. Johnny was sprawled on top of Dobbsy with three bullet holes going diagonally down his huge back.

"Johnny!" shouts me and Lem at the same time, running into the room. We had to step over a body, which turns out to be Doctor Peters, his neck snapped and his eyes rolled back in his head. That was Johnny's work fer sure.

We pull Johnny offa Dobbsy, and he's cold and white, with the glazed, half-open eyes of a dead man. Abel leans down to look at Dobbs, but me and Lem turn away—it was too much to have to see two of your best friends like that at once, specially knowing Dobbsy wasn't able to defend himself and Johnny died trying to protect him, shot in the back almost point-blank.

"Hey, this feller's still breathin'!" says one of Kearny's men, who had his ear down next to Johnny's mouth. I run over and put my hand over Johnny's chest, and wha'dya know, that sledge-hammer of a heart of his was still going. It was weak, but it was still going.

"Jesus H. Christ!" I shout, "Somebody go run for a doctor!"

Another of Kearny's men says he'll go and runs out. I was so surprised and so wore out that suddenly I just fell back on my ass and sat there, dazed and not seeing or hearing nothing for a few minutes. Then I notice Lem across the room dancing a goddamn jig, and that sorta wakes me up.

"Lem," I says, taking a deep breath, "just what in hell d'ya think you're doing over there? You lost your mind?"

Lem don't say nothing, he just comes dancing over to me, pulls me to my feet, and spins me around to face the bed Dobbsy's on. And what do I see but Abel dabbing Dobbsy's forehead with a wet cloth and Dobbsy smiling up at me. Then Lem starts dancing me around the room, and soon I found I was dancing all on my own. I never felt happier—or more strange—than right then.

So we finally come to our senses, and an hour or so later the doctor—a real one this time—shows up and starts looking after Johnny and Dobbs. Johnny was in rough shape, having lost a lotta blood, but you just knowed he was gonna pull through. And Dobbsy, who somehow survived being beat up, starved, and poisoned, was just strong enough to say, "Johnny?" When we told him Johnny was gonna make it, he let out a big sigh, closed his eyes, and went to sleep again. I reckoned once this thing was over, Dobbsy wasn't gonna sleep for a month straight.

We went out to the kitchen, and Bill Kearny was there talking to Abel.

"Thanks for not givin' up on an old block-head like me," says Kearny, shaking Abel's hand. "Once I get an idea in my thick skull, there's nothin' on this earth to get it out again."

"Forget it, Bill," says Abel. "Red had a lot of people fooled, me included. No hard feelings."

"And, hey," says Kearny, "I'm real sorry about your pa. He was a good man."

"Yeah," says Abel, looking away. "Thanks."

We did a final head count, and it turns out there was eleven of Red's men laying dead in the house and three more wounded. Only one of 'em was in any state to be asked questions, and he was one of them two we fed to the ants and left locked up in the shed—ol' Fat Face.

"So," says Abel, standing over him as the doctor bandaged up the hole he had in his arm, "we meet again."

"Yeah, lucky me," he says. "Ain't I taken enough abuse from you?"

"Yesterday, when we had our little chat, you

forgot to mention Red was the big boss," says Abel.

"You didn't ask me nothin' about Red," says Fat Face. "You ask me where Randy was, and I told you."

"Whatever," says Abel. "Now I'm asking you about Red. And Slim. Where are they? And please, I don't want to have to disturb those poor ants again."

When Fat Face hears the word "ants," he starts looking like he was gonna lose his lunch.

"Hey, don't even joke about that," he says. "You know, my partner never did recover from that. He lost his mind out there in the shed. I had to . . . shut him up. Anyway, if you know where the Comanches are, you should be able to find Red— or what's left of him. He took the rest of the men and set off about an hour before you hit us. We was only a diversion. But I was happier'n a pig in shit to stay behind and shoot it out with some white men. See? I got a doctor lookin' after me and everything. Real civilized. Now, if I'da went with Red and the rest of them poor slobs, right about now some Comanche squaw would be slicin' me up into little pieces to decorate the teepee with."

"How many men did Red take with him?" says Abel.

"I dunno," says Fat Face. "Maybe twenty, thirty."

Abel tells some of Kearny's men to stay at the house overnight in case Red doubles back and then turns to the doctor.

"Hey, Doc," he says, picking up his hat and nodding at Fat Face, "don't spend too much time on this one—he's not long for this world. Let's go, boys. You ready?"

12

We got some fresh horses—the ones we was using before still warn't back from wherever they run off to during the shoot-out—and hit the trail again. Soon, we was riding full speed again, and I don't mind telling you my ass and legs was falling-off sore, but there warn't nothing for it. Once we dealt with Red, there'd be plenty of time for sitting around being bored all day.

As we got near to Many Horses' village, we got the same armed escort as before. Them warriors was getting used to us, I reckon, 'cause one of 'em kinda smiles when he sees us. There hadn't been no attack on the camp itself. We kinda figured Red would try storming the Sacred Place direct anyway. But we warn't about to show up there without Many Horses at our side. Without his influence, them Comanche sentries wouldn't care which white men we was.

So we rode out to the canyon with Many Horses and, when we got there, we saw right away what'd happened. Red's men was all layin' dead in a circle of dead horses at the bottom of the canyon, which meant the Comanches let 'em ride straight into the place and then swooped down on 'em. The men musta shot their own horses to use as wall, but they was outnumbered, outgunned, and outsmarted, so the Comanches just took their time and finished 'em off one by one. We looked over the bodies and found Slim, his mouth and eyes wide open in terror. But there was no sign of Red.

"The damn coward," says Lem. "Always lettin' someone else take on the dangerous stuff and sneakin' out the back way when it don't work out."

"That's all right," says Abel, walking back to his horse. "Maybe I'll still get a crack at him."

"Who is this man you seek?" says Many Horses.

"He is my father's brother, Many Horses," says Abel. "He not only killed those travelers and farmers the other day, but also my father."

"I see. After killing his own brother, it must have been easy for him to kill the others," says Many Horses.

"I guess you're right," says Abel. "Anyway, your Sacred Place is safe again."

"Perhaps, but for how long?" says Many Horses. "Once word got out among your people that there was gold here, it was the beginning of the end for the Sacred Place. My warriors won today, but what of tomorrow?"

"I think I have an answer, Many Horses, but you will have to trust me," says Abel. "You will have to trust me with the lives of all your people."

Many Horses stood silent for a minute, thinking about it, I guess.

"Very well, Abel Braddock," he says. "I will trust you, because I know you are not a man who cares only for his own skin. What is this answer you speak of?"

"First," says Abel, "I will take the gold that is in the cave and exchange it for regular money. You see, that gold is valuable because it is gold, but it is even more valuable because it is very old."

Many Horses kinda screws up his face for a second, then he smiles.

"I think I understand, Abel Braddock," he says. "It becomes more valuable the older it gets, just as the legend of the Sacred Place became more powerful over time. How very interesting."

"That's right," says Abel. "And I will use the money to buy as much of the land in this area as it will buy, and that land will be for the use of your people alone. Also, I will give you part of my ranch to use, the large northern portion where there is a river and plenty of game. I do not need all of the land I own, er, all of the land I have been *using*, so you are welcome to it. I can't guarantee it'll work forever, the way things are heading, and all, but—"

"I understand, Abel Braddock," says Many Horses, putting his hand on Abel's shoulder. "No man can change the future. But if we leave the gold where it is, it will be taken from us before very long, and then we will have nothing. I will do as you say. You are a good friend to my people. And I promise you there will be only peace between us, even after I am gone. I swear it."

The two men shook hands. Then Many Horses yelled something to his warriors, and one by one they all come up and start shaking our hands, only they didn't quite have the hang of it 'cause one huge feller nearly pulls my arm out of its socket. But he had got such a big smile going that I didn't wanta spoil it by telling him he was doing it all wrong. Then we said good-byes all around, told Many Horses we'd be back in a few days to pick up where we left off, and headed back to Elsinore.

In the morning, Abel tells the men who stayed over that the ranch was sorely in need of help now that they was all dead or in jail, so they was gonna go out and find as many able-bodied men in Gonzago as wanted work and send 'em all back to get started on turning Elsinore back into a cattle ranch again. Then Abel says he's going to look up Jimbo McCullock in the jail and see what he can do for him, and I says I'll go with him.

So just the two of us headed on into Gonzago again. When we got there, we run into Wendel, who could barely look Abel in the eye on account of he heard about what happened, but Abel told

him to snap out of it and forget the whole business, and right away Wendel was his old self
again. Then we headed up to the jailhouse and
knocked on the sheriff's door.

There warn't no answer, so we walk in, and
there's Sheriff Wellman, lying stone-cold dead on
the floor in a dried-up pool of his own blood.
Here we go again, I thought.

Abel doesn't say nothing, just runs around to
where the cells are and then comes walking back
out again real slow.

"Jimbo's dead, too," says Abel, slumping
down into a chair. "Boyd, this, this is all my
fault."

"Oh, now don't start that, Abel," I says,
standing up. "Nothing you done's got anything to
do with these crazy people. You might as well say
you never shoulda plugged Randy's old man back
when. If you hadn't, you'd be dead, and them
Indians woulda had no one to turn to. Forget
them, what about us—me and Lem and Johnny
and Dobbsy and Bill? Huh? If you'da checked
out before the war even started, none of us
woulda made it through alive, now would we?
And that goes for a helluva lotta other fellers in
our outfit, too. So just remember that next time
you're feeling responsible for all this crap. Like
Many Horses says, no man can predict the
future."

Abel looks up at me with hollow eyes. I
thought he was about to take out his pistol and
shut me up.

"Boyd," he says, "when did you get so god-damn gabby? At least let me enjoy the break from Dobbsy for another day or so."

I smile, and he smiles back, and I felt a whole lot better.

"Aw, isn't that sweet," says a woman's voice from behind a cabinet in the corner. "Two friends sharing a laugh over a dead body."

"Daphne?" says Abel. "I wondered where you had gotten to. Well, are you satisfied now? Or won't you be happy until every single person in this town is dead?"

As she steps out from behind the cabinet, Daphne starts laughing her head off. She looked worse than Sheriff Wellman. And she was carrying a gun.

"Boyd, you darling man," she says, "did you tell Abel here about our little secret? Abel, Boyd and Johnny and I are having an affair behind your back, aren't we Boyd?"

"That's nice, Daphne," says Abel, "but let's stay on the subject, shall we? Just what do you want? If you wanted to kill me, why dance around all this time? Why not just put a bullet in me. You seem to enjoy doing that to people."

"Hey, Abel," I says. "Don't give her any ideas."

"Daphne, listen," says Abel, "you're not well. You need to rest, to get better. Just put the gun down and let's end all this, now. I promise you won't have to go to jail."

"Oh, spare me, Abel," she says. "I know

exactly what I'm doing, you pathetic bag of wind. Talk, talk, talk, that's you. Always talking the nerve out of people. You think it's because they can't help themselves in the face of your brilliant, inescapable logic, but it's not that at all. It's that you bore them silly, and they just go limp after a while! Well, I prefer action. An eye for an eye, that's for me. Can you imagine how hard that must have been for me, having to wait all those years to settle up with you? Anyway, you can save your lame sympathy speech. As if I'd let you take this gun out of my shaking little hand and burst into tears. Ha!"

"Fine, Daphne, if that's the way you want it," says Abel, cool as ever. "Then before you shoot me, let me just say this. The only thing I enjoyed more than watching Randy get a picture window through his chest was the look on your father's face as he fell to the ground realizing he had his holster on backwards."

Now that there was vintage Dobbsy, not Abel at all, so I guessed he was deliberately trying to get her so mad she couldn't shoot straight or something. Well, she was mad, all right. She didn't say nothing; she just turned beet red and lunged at Abel, screaming her head off.

She crashes into Abel, and down they go onto the floor. She's trying to point her gun to his face, and he's trying to wrestle it outta her hand. I reckon he musta got her a mite too angry, 'cause Abel's a fairly big man, and there she was, holding her own as they rolled around.

Suddenly, things ain't going so well for Abel. His hand slips offa the gun, and for a second Daphne's got control of it. She jams it into Abel's mouth and pulls the trigger just as I'm drawing on her, but Abel's hand whips down, and somehow he gets a finger between the hammer and the firing pin. Never seen anything closer than that. But then she wrenches it away and starts bringing it around toward his face again, and I decide I had enough of this and I fire, blowing the back off her head.

Her body twitched around some for a second or two, and then she finally went limp. It didn't bother me none, 'cause in those moments she warn't a woman no more, or even a human being, but an animal, a crazed, foaming-at-the-mouth dog that had to be shot down.

Abel pushes her offa him like she was a big bag of manure or something and rolls away, getting slowly to his feet.

"Jesus, Boyd," he says, dusting himself off. "What the hell took you so long? She almost had me there, a couple of times. What were you thinking, letting her get that thing all the way into my mouth, for God's sake?"

I reckon it warn't bothering him none that she was dead, neither. Only he was kinda mad at himself that he didn't take care of her earlier, like he shoulda done with Randy. But it was over.

Well, Daphne sure made a mess of things, killing the sheriff like that, and it mighta been tight for us trying to explain everything to the

marshall we sent for from San Angelo if it warn't
for the fact that we had about a hundred witnesses in Gonzago who'd swear to what a buncha
wackos Red and them Eckhardts was and what
they been up to the last week. And as for Red, he
was still at large, as they say, only now he was
more of a wanted man than any of them fellers he
hired. The marshall promised that, wherever he
turned up, he'd do all he could to make sure they
brought him back to our district to hang him on
account of how many people's lives he messed up
in the area.

So after we saw to poor old Jimbo's funeral,
which everyone in town showed up for outta
respect for Abel, we started back into the ranch-
ing business again. And, believe me, after having
Red in charge for a while, we sure had our work
cut out for us. Abel even had to hire a coupla pro-
fessional ranchers to come down from Abilene
and show him how to get things going right again.
But the local men all wanted to work for Abel
now, so there was no shortage of help, and soon
the place bore a striking resemblance to a ranch
once again. We all settled into our chores again.
We was all so busy trying to make things work for
Abel that we didn't have the time to think about
what a godawful bore it all was, least not for a
while.

Johnny made a complete recovery in a few
weeks, just as we suspected he would. And he
mighta been a few bricks shy of a load, but he
was a natural born rancher, and when the profes-

sional help left, Johnny become Abel's first foreman. We was all real happy at first, thinking we
had it made having a pal of ours as boss, but during working hours it was like Johnny never heard
of us before, driving us as hard as any other cowhand. 'Course, we complained about him, calling
him all kindsa names, and Dobbs kept saying he
knowed Johnny only saved his life so's he could
torture him for the next forty years. But we didn't
mind, really, on account of how he was only doing
his job after all.

Abel kept his word to Many Horses, naturally, and had the cattle and fencing cleared outta
that river bottom area for the Comanches to use,
keeping only a downstream portion to run water
off of for the ranch. And he took that Spanish
gold and turned it into a ton of money, so much,
in fact, that after buying up all the adjoining land
that was available, there was still plenty left over,
which he put into a bank for Many Horses' tribe
to use as they needed. But Abel did keep one of
them coins and gave it to me to replace the good
luck piece. This one warn't all worn smooth, at
least not till I had it for a while.

Dobbsy told me them Spanish skeletons in
the cave was prob'ly members of a whole army
that come to America hundreds of years ago with
a feller name of Coronado, and they brought
enough gold along to use for trade and for brib-
ing Indian tribes to fight against each other—
that was the idea, anyway. Well, them Spanish
soldier's must've took a wrong turn somewhere,

getting cut off from the main army. Apparently, they was looking for some big gold mine or something that didn't exist, and I thought that was kinda funny, that the only gold in the area turns out to be what they had with 'em.

13

Well, I wish that was the end of my story, but it ain't, not quite. Abel kept running his ranch for about fifteen years, turning a nice profit and keeping everything friendly with the local Comanches, even after Many Horses died. Johnny, Dobbs and Bill stayed on—that's how I knowed about what happened later, Bill told me when I run into him years later. Me and Lem, we took off a couple years after we arrived at Elsinore, and we separated after a few months on account of him meeting a real sweetheart of a girl in New Mexico and getting married, if you can believe that.

When that happened, I decided to finally try my hand at gold prospecting, but I never found a single ounce of the stuff, not in eight years of trying, off and on. I was like them Spanish fellers in a way, 'cause that lucky piece I carried with me

was the only gold I ever managed to get my
hands on. No matter how down and out I ever
got, I never gave in to the urge to sell the damn
thing. Prob'ly coulda made a couple hundred
bucks on it. But now that I'm old, I'm awful glad
I didn't, 'cause it's a real memento of some wild
times.

Anyhow, what happened was fifteen years
later, Abel was leading a cattle drive up to
Kansas, and one night, he left his men in charge
of the herd and rode by himself into some little
town I can't even remember the name of, way up
north at the top of Texas. He's having a drink in
the local watering hole, and some scraggly looking feller just walks up from behind and shoots
him. Abel turns around and gets off a shot before
he falls down and dies, and he gets the feller
right in the face and kills him.

No one in town ever saw him before, but the
feller turns out to be Red Braddock, who somehow managed to evade the law for fifteen years.
It was crazy to think Red coulda drifted into that
little one-horse town at the same time as Abel
shows up. Just the worst kinda luck a man could
have. Until I heard the story from Bill, oh, ten
years ago now, I always figured they got Red and
hung him, and that Abel musta lived happily ever
after. But I guess things don't always work out
the way they oughta. And that's my story.

NOVELS RIPPED STRAIGHT FROM THE PAGES OF AMERICAN HISTORY

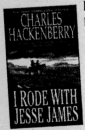

I RODE WITH JESSE JAMES
by Charles Hackenberry
Spur Award-Winning Author

Despite his promise to bring him to justice, ex-con Willie Goodwin is drawn to the charasmatic Jesse James, the clan's reckless lifestyle . . . and James's beautiful cousin. As the pressure of the law closes in, Goodwin gallops to an inevitable showdown where only the lucky will survive.

• Also available . . . **FRIENDS**

RIDE FOR RIMFIRE
by Hank Edwards

Only Rimfire's foreman, Shell Harper, can save the famous ranch and pass its title to the true heir, Emmy Gunnison. To do so he must stand alone against the infamous Billy Bishop gang, as the last hope for Rimfire.

• Also available . . . **APACHE SUNDOWN**

MOUNTAIN CAPTIVE
by John Legg

The winter of 1834-35 is nearly over, and Jim Blackwood and his partners are preparing to leave Cache Valley for the spring hunt. Just before they strike camp, the warlike Blackfeet sweep over them, capturing Blackwood's wife. Now he wants revenge, and he'll fight to the death to get it.   (Available in December)

• Also available . . . **BUCKSKIN VENGEANCE** and **SOUTHWEST THUNDER**

BLOOD OF TEXAS
by Will Camp

As a Mexican living in San Antonio in 1835, Rubio Portillo despised the heartless Mexican rule, and wants to fight instead for the freedom of Texas. When troops attack the Alamo, Rubio will have to struggle to gain acceptance as a loyal Texan while battling his own friends and family.

AN ORDINARY MAN
by J.R. McFarland

A drifting lawman with a knack for killing, MacLane was a lonely man—until an odd twist changed his fate. Only then did he have the chance to change the course of his life and become an ordinary man with an extraordinary message to deliver.